NEVER KILL
A TEXAS RANGER!

The rule was hard not to break, Fargo thought bitterly, ten hours after he had been penned up in the cave like a trapped cougar. When darkness came there was a slim chance that he could blast his way past the Rangers who were keeping him there. But the fact remained that anyone who killed a Texas Ranger was doomed. The force would never rest until it killed you.

So how was he going to get out of this cave? The Rangers outnumbered him six to one, and they had food and water. Should he let himself be driven out by hunger and thirst—or start shooting and make himself a marked man for life?

We will send you a free catalog on request. Any titles not in your local book store can be purchased by mail. Send the price of the book plus 50¢ shipping charge to Tower Books, P.O. Box 511, Murray Hill Station, New York, N.Y. 10156-0511.

Titles currently in print are available for industrial and sales promotion at reduced rates. Address inquiries to Tower Publications, Inc., Two Park Avenue, New York, New York 10016, Attention: Premium Sales Department.

FARGO #9:
THE
SHARPSHOOTERS

John Benteen

TOWER BOOKS ▌ NEW YORK CITY

OTHER BOOKS IN THE FARGO SERIES

A TOWER BOOK

Published by

Tower Publications, Inc.
Two Park Avenue
New York, N.Y. 10016

Copyright © MCMLXX by John Benteen

Chapter I

Mounted on tall, sleek mules, they came down out of the wild reaches of the Davis Mountains, thirty of them, in a winding column. Behind them creaked two springless wagons covered with tarpaulins, drawn by plodding, sharp-horned oxen. Filing past the decaying buildings of old Fort Davis, under the towering rock pile of Sleeping Lion Mountain, they entered the little town that bore the fort's name. The hooves of their mounts stirred a stream of dust that the wind whipped down the short main street. As they rode by, Fargo watched them keenly, sizing them up as fighters, appraising the small arsenal of weapons with which each man was armed.

They were big, lean men, wide in the shoulder, deep in the chest, rawboned and weather beaten. Because they were all fathers and sons, brothers and cousins, and had interbred for generations, the resemblance among them was startling. The blue eyes, hawk noses, thin, steel-trap mouths, the long tow-colored hair and beards and mustaches—these were general. Some wore range garb, some bib overalls like farmers. All, without exception, wore black slouch hats, and all had gunbelts strapped around their waists. And every one of them carried a long gun across his saddle bow. It was the long guns that made Fargo's eyes kindle. Most of them were single shot rifles. And the majority of those were long-barreled, short-stocked guns of antique manufacture—Kentucky rifles, squirrel rifles they were sometimes called, not much different from the sort of weapon used by Daniel Boone or the oldtime mountain men who had, in search of beaver, opened up the West almost a hundred years before. Those so armed wore powder horns and bullet pouches slung across their bodies. The ones who balanced Sharps fifty-caliber buffalo guns before them had cartridge bandoliers draped around their torsos. And there were those who favored double barreled, big-bore shotguns; and shells for these clacked in similar shoulder belts. Fargo rolled a cigar across his mouth. This was his first look at the Canfields. *No,* he thought now. *No, it ain't worth it. Twenty thousand dollars isn't enough to take on that bunch of fighting men and kill them all.*

As they swept on by with a jingle of gear and a steady drum of hooves, he took another look at the big man riding at the column's head: the patriarch. Roaring Tom Canfield, chieftain of the clan, tall in his saddle despite his sixty-odd years, blue eyes like ice beneath the black slouch hat, silver beard falling halfway to his belt, a mane of iron-gray hair shagging down his neck to his shoulders. Roaring Tom wore a homespun shirt and woolen pants and high, black, flat-heeled boots. A powder horn and bullet pouch were draped across his body from left to right; a braided leather loop supported a steer's big horn with a trumpet's mouthpiece on his other flank. The long-barreled rifle across his saddle was a marvel of workmanship, its cherrywood stock and fore end inlaid with hammered silver. A huge Bowie knife rode in a leather sheath on his left hip; a Colt Navy revolver was snugly holstered on his right.

Then he reined in his mule, lifted himself in his stirrups, scanned the street with those ice-blue eyes. They came to rest on Fargo, lingered, appraising this stranger in town, this tall man lounging against the front of the single saloon who showed such interest in the column. They ran up and down Fargo's body, missing nothing, taking in the battered old cavalry campaign hat perched jauntily on close-cropped hair gone prematurely white, the hard, surpassingly ugly face, weathered, tanned, battle-scarred: a face that women never failed to look at more than once and which was like a danger signal to men who could read the violence which lay behind it. They inventoried the wide shoulders and flat belly and trim hips and horseman's legs; the Colt .38 Officer's Model revolver in its holster on his hip, the cavalry boots and spurs beneath untucked khaki pants. Something kindled in those eyes: respect and caution. For a moment they met Fargo's gray ones, deepset beneath pale brows under buttresses of bone. Then they slid away, and Fargo knew that Roaring Tom had him tagged with the accuracy of long experience: fighting man, dangerous, one to watch.

The old man kept his mule tight-gathered, said something to the rider on the big sorrel beside him. That one looked at Fargo, too. Not over twenty-three or four, except for his youth and lack of beard, he was a carbon copy of the patriarch and had to be his son. His eyes, too, meet Fargo's, and something flared in them instantly: challenge. Fargo tensed.

9

Like a young bull, he thought. On the prod, ready to fight any time, any place, anybody or anything that'll fight him. This, he figured, would be Jess, the one Steed and Hanna had warned him about. Next to Roaring Tom, he was the most dangerous of the clan.

Then the old man unslung the steerhorn trumpet, raised it to his lips, blew a short blast. The sound echoed, loud and mournfully, from the rock walls that backed the town. At his signal, the rest of the column halted, strung out along the street. Men dismounted, cradling their rifles or shotguns in their arms, hitched their horses. But the wagons came on to stop opposite Fargo and the bar. From beneath the hooped canvas of the one in the lead, two women climbed out and went down over the wheels, awkwardly, in long gingham skirts that dragged the dust.

At first, their sunbonnets concealed their faces. Then they turned. One was a withered crone, but the other—Fargo took his cigar from his mouth. He was looking into eyes as blue as those of the men, but a different kind of blue, warm, cornflower blue, set in a triangular face of delicacy and loveliness. He could just see the glint of bright blond hair tucked up beneath the bonnet; he did not miss the wide, full-lipped, sensual mouth. Nor the swell of large breasts beneath the bodice of the old-fashioned dress, mounds full and proud beneath the cloth. There was an instant when her gaze met his; what he saw in it was not the hostility the men had shown, but a sudden, flaring, bold interest. For a second they looked at one another, the girl frozen, rigid, beside the wagon wheel. Then the old woman saw Fargo and her face twisted in a snarl. She seized the girl's arm, led her behind the wagon and toward the drygoods store across the street.

10

Fargo turned away and went inside the bar. Steed and Hanna were standing at the window, looking out. "All right," Steed said. "You've seen 'em, now. Let's go back there and strike our deal." Without waiting for Fargo to answer, he led the way to the little private room in back, where their bottle and glasses were on the table.

Jim Hanna closed the door, pulled out a chair with a booted foot. He was in his sixties, too, lean and tough as rawhide, and owner of one of the biggest ranches in this part of Texas. Walt Steed's spread was not much smaller. Steed was younger, in his forties, heavy-set, running to fat. There was something about him Fargo did not like, an arrogance, as if everyone should defer to him because of his wealth and power. "All right," he said again. "That's the lot of 'em, Fargo. Now, our deal—"

"There won't be any deal," Fargo said.

They looked at him in amazement. He sat down, smiling faintly, poured himself a drink. Steed and Hanna dropped into chairs. "What the hell you mean, no deal? Twenty thousand dollars—?"

"Isn't enough."

Hanna fiddled with his white mustache. "Now, wait a minute. We heard Neal Fargo was the best free-lance gunman left above the Rio. And that he would do anything for money—"

"Maybe some of what you heard was wrong," Fargo said quietly. "I make my living with guns, yeah. But I'm not a hired killer. A man's got a job he wants done, if it's a fighting job, I'll take it on, provided the pay is right. And once I give my word to do it, if I got to kill somebody to get it done—" He spread his hands. "Well, that's part of the game. But what you want me to do is go out in those mountains and assassinate thirty men, knock 'em off

11

one by one, backshoot 'em, drygulch 'em, pick 'em off like coyotes—"

"That's right," Steed said. "The way Tom Horn knocked off those nesters up in Wyoming."

"They hanged Tom Horn," Neal Fargo said.

"Well, Tom Horn wasn't the fighting man you are. They say you've done everything. You were in the Rough Riders in the Spanish-American War, the cavalry in the Philippines during the Insurrection there. You've tried the gold fields in Alaska, you've been a professional prize fighter, a gambler, a logger, worked in the oil fields. And, God knows, you've been mixed up in enough revolutions down in Mexico and Central America. There ain't nobody can beat you with those guns of yours, that Colt, that Winchester; and, most of all, that sawed-off riot gun they say you like to use. That's what we've heard; that when there was trouble, Neal Fargo's the man you want. And that's why we asked you to come to see us—"

"All that's true," Fargo said. "You left out a few things." He grinned, coldly, like a wolf. "I've done my share of cowpunching, too, and one time I was even a bouncer in a whorehouse in Baton Rouge when things got tough. But even being a bouncer in a whorehouse beats being a paid backshooter."

Jim Hanna's lips thinned. He leaned forward across the table. "All right, it's a nasty proposition. But we understood you weren't picky. I don't like the idea, either, but we've reached a point where we can't afford pickiness ourselves."

He poured a drink. "Those damned Canfields," he grated. "They got no business here anyhow. They should have stayed back in those North Carolina mountains where they come from. The people back in those hills are a hundred years behind the times,

12

and so're the Canfields, with their corn-whiskey makin' and their blood feuds."

"It was their feud with another clan, the Whipples, that got 'em run out of North Carolina," Steed added. "Nobody even knows what started that dispute, but those two hillbilly families been at war with one another for fifty years, shootin' each other from ambush, killin' each other on sight. All because of some insult that didn't amount to a hill of beans to begin with. Anyhow, the Whipples finally got the upper hand. They got into politics and used their power to force the Canfields out of them hills. They had one last big fight, the Canfields shot hell out of the Whipples and then took off west."

"I know all that," Fargo said.

"And we've already told you the rest," Hanna added. "How the Canfields showed up here two years ago, moved into the Davis Mountains. The whole damned family, thirty fighting men and all their wives and daughters and little kids, just took over Black Valley up there, the best rangeland and water in this part of the country, squatted on it, and then—" His voice crackled with anger. "Then started plowin' up the grass to grow corn to make their damned moonshine whiskey with."

"And you and Steed had been runnin' cattle in there and they forced you out." Fargo lit another cigar. "You didn't hold title to the land—"

"Neither do the Canfields. Title's all tied up in court; Indian claims, Spanish land grants, and the Federal government tryin' to claim it belongs to them. It was anybody's land, and it was worth a fortune to us as summer graze."

Fargo chuckled without much humor. "And the two of you—worth God knows how much money, and with more than fifty riders apiece. You couldn't throw 'em out?"

"Don't think we wouldn't like to," Hanna rasped. "There's nothin' Walt and I would like better than to put together an army and go in there and just rub all of 'em out, the way we used to do it in the old days. But the old days are gone. We try it now, we'd have the Rangers and the Army down on us before you could spit. On top of which, you can't hire gunhands any more the way you used to. There ain't enough of 'em left. And ordinary cowboys won't go up against the Canfields for their fifty a month and found."

"Anyhow, Black Valley's a natural fort," Steed said. "Only one entrance, through Black Canyon, and that's a damned trap. Thirty men, all sharpshooters like the Canfields—those people can knock the eye out of a squirrel at a hundred yards with them damned antique muzzle-loaders of theirs—could stand off an army. No. The only way is for one man to sneak in there. One man that knows how to fight Injun style—like you. As good at long-range shootin' as any Canfield, and who could pick 'em off from ambush one by one, the way you'd kill rats in a barn."

"And get out again," put in Hanna. "Without leavin' any tracks. Nothin' to connect him—or us—to the shootin's. Goddamn it, Fargo, we want that range. And we're willin' to pay you a fortune to get it back for us. Twenty thousand dollars is a lot of money."

"Not really," Fargo said.

They both stared at him.

"That's about what I figure on earnin', minimum, on any job I take on. Not hardly ever less, sometimes more. And sometimes I do two jobs a year or even three. In between spells of work, I like high living. Good liquor, high-stakes gambling, and . . ." he smiled, "women. The best women. They come

14

high. Not that I pay 'em, but if they're good to me. I'm good to them, spend money on 'em. That's where my money goes, and it goes fast. The point is, though, that twenty thousand dollars ain't all that big to me. Especially now."

"What do you mean, especially now?" asked Hanna.

Fargo gestured carelessly. "The revolution in Mexico's still goin' full blast. Time was when the *revolucionarios* could buy guns and ammo freely in the United States. Now the government's laid down an embargo on sales to 'em. That shoots the price way up. I can run one load of ammunition across the Rio to Villa and make as much in two weeks as you folks want to pay me for this job of yours. And at a hell of a lot less risk."

"Risk? You got to dodge the Rangers, the Army, the Border Patrol. You got to dodge the Mexican government's army, bandits—"

"Yeah," Fargo said. "But that's better than the Canfields."

"What?"

"I'm a man who plays the odds. I like the big money. I figure the risks to get it, take what's necessary, not one bit more. Right now, I can make more with less risk running guns and ammo to the Mexicans."

He drank, poured another shot, and jerked his thumb toward the street. "I watched 'em come in for their supplies and to sell their whiskey. I sized 'em up. Not that I really had to; I spent a stretch in those Caroline mountains of theirs one time, and I know what kind of men they breed. Mountains breed the toughest men there are. If you're their friend, they'll lay down their lives for you. But if you insult 'em, even so much as spit on one of em's boots, much less hurt one of their kinfolk or mess

15

with their women, then you got to fight the whole damned family. Right down to the last man. They'll declare a blood feud against you and come after you and you got to kill 'em all, right down to the last little kid that's old enough to raise a gun and aim it. If you don't, sooner or later they'll get you."

"That's what we want you to do. Wipe 'em all out."

"Even to the young-uns," Steed added. "Nits breed lice."

Fargo's mouth twisted. He stood up. "No, thanks, gentlemen. Kill your own snakes. I got business across the Rio Grande."

"So you're afraid," Steed said cuttingly. "The great Neal Fargo's afraid of a bunch of hillbillies."

Fargo turned, slowly, and stared at him with gray eyes like flakes of cold iron. Steed's face paled, he pushed back his chair under that terrible gaze. Then Fargo let out a long breath. His ugly face relaxed. "Steed, I only fight for money. It's my stock in trade and I don't give anything away free, not even when a man badmouths me. But I wouldn't try it twice if I were you. I might break one of my own rules and pistolwhip the hell out of you."

He took his cigar from his mouth. "I'll lead an army or run a revolution or run guns or do anything else I can to make a buck. And God help anybody who tries to stop me. But I don't bushwhack men I don't even know, who've done nothin' to me, for lousy pay. Not unless I'm a hell of a lot hungrier than I've ever been. I've got nothin' against the Canfields and they've nothin' against me, and I'm content to leave it that way. If, sometimes, when I'm on business of my own, they get crossways of me, that's a different matter. But when I become a hired assassin, it'll only be because I'm too old and feeble to stay alive any other way. I ain't old and

16

feeble yet. So long, Steed. Hanna. Thanks for the whiskey." Then he turned, walked out.

Just past the back room's door, he halted. The main barroom was not large; and right now it was thronged with gun-hung Canfields. Roaring Tom, standing to one side, was directing the others as they lugged in case after case of quart fruit jars of clear, white liquid or rolled in kegs filled with the same potent homemade corn whiskey. "Now, look sharp, thar, you, Bert, Sam, Willie. Don't you trip and throw ye'se'f down with them 'ere jugs. Take it gentle with that 'ere kaig, Joe Junior." They hauled the stuff into another back room and stacked it. Festooned with powder horn, shot case, and steer-horn trumpet, squirrel rifle cradled in his arm, the old man strode to the bar. "Thar y'are, Mister Forrest. Thet thar's all prime corn, second and third run, copper still. I'll take our money now, iffn ye please."

"Yes, sir." The proprietor counted out double eagles, shoved them across the bar. Roaring Tom frowned, sorting through them. Then he barked: "Jess!"

"Yes, Pappy." The big young man joined him at the bar. He was, Fargo saw, one of the few who carried a repeating rifle, an ancient, long-barreled Henry.

"Maybe my head fer figgers ain't too good today. Count thet thar money and see whut ye come out with."

Jess's thin lips moved as he went through the pile of gold. Then he slowly raised his head. "I make hit a hunderd and ninety dollars Pappy."

"Thet's whut I got, too," said Roaring Tom. "Mr. Forrest."

Forrest was a short, plump, pale man whose

round face went even paler. "I shoulda told you first, Mr. Canfield. There's been a drop in the price of whiskey. We get the best Kentucky bourbon in now for fifty cents a gallon less than it cost last month."

"Oh, do ye now?" Roaring Tom's voice was deep, yet soft. "Well, Kaintucky bourbon ain't Canfield corn. We ain't cut our price none."

"All the same, I can't afford—"

"I figger we're thutty dollar short." Roaring Tom looked at him a moment. Then he sighed. "All right, boys. Haul hit back out and put hit in the wagon."

"Yeah, you heard Pappy," Jess barked. "Go git thet whiskey and load hit up."

"Now, wait a minute, Mr. Canfield. That's a fair price. Especially since if you don't sell it here, you'll have to haul it another fifty miles."

"Thet ain't the point," Canfield said. "The point is, we done set our price and we aim to git hit. Even if we got to haul hit clear back across the Mississippi River. I don't care whut ye pay fer thet Kaintucky cat pee, thar ain't no whiskey made thet's good as Canfield corn. It's wuth whut we git fer hit, and we don't take no less." He shoved the gold back across the counter. "Thar's your money, Mister Forrest. Looks like we won't do no more business."

"Now, there ain't no reason for you to be so touchy. Dadblame it, Canfield, it'll cost you twice thirty dollars, three times to—" He looked into Canfield's eyes, broke off. "All right," he said bitterly. "Here's your extra thirty dollars. When the cowboys come in on payday, they don't want nothin' but Canfield corn. They'll pay extra for it, have to now, I reckon."

Canfield took the money. "Canfield liquor's worth extra. Mr. Forrest, lemme give ye a leetle bit of advice. Don't ye ever try to shortchange us again,

18

ye hyar me? Next time ye do, we're likely to fergit our raisin' and jest mortally tear this hyar place of yourn plumb apart." He spat tobacco juice into the sawdust on the floor. "Sharp business is one thing. But cheatin's another. One thing us Canfields cain't abide is a cheat." He took the coins, dropped them into his shot pouch. "Feller'd do well to recollect thet in the future. Might help him to stay healthy."

Forrest mopped cold sweat from his forehead. "Yes, sir," he whispered. "Yes, sir, Mr. Canfield. I didn't mean to git your feathers ruffled."

"They don't ruffle easy. But when they do, they stay ruffled. Ye b'ar thet in mind, Mr. Forrest. All right, boys. Tote the stuff on back thar." He turned, hitching at his gunbelt. His eyes met Fargo's again, for an instant. Then he went out, boots clumping on the board floor. Jess followed him, shooting a ferocious glance at Forrest, and the others filed out behind him.

When they were gone, Fargo went to the bar. "Let me have a shot of that Canfield corn."

"Sure." Forrest looked toward the swinging doors, lowered his voice. "They are the damndest people to do business with I ever seen."

"Maybe they expect a man to keep his word," Fargo said.

Forrest looked at him keenly, a little apprehensively. "Good God, you ain't a Canfield, too?"

"In most ways, no," said Fargo. "In some ways, yes. The drink."

Forrest poured it. Fargo held it to his nose, sniffed it. Good corn whiskey had a mellow bouquet; bad corn, poison moonshine, was so rank no man in his right mind could get it to his mouth if he smelled it first. This whiskey caressed his nostrils with its odor. He drank, found it raw, yet oddly smooth. It went down, exploded in his belly like a bomb's detonation.

"That," he said, in sincere tribute, "is drinkin' whiskey." He smacked his lips, hitched at his gunbelt, turned, and went out on the street, still crowded with Canfields.

Neal Fargo had ridden into town on a big bay gelding he'd bought in Del Rio. For his conference with Steed and Hanna, he'd tethered it outside the one general store of this little town, seat of an enormous, sprawling county. When the Apaches had been rampant, Fort Davis had been an important army post, but once the Indians were quelled and it, no longer needed, had been abandoned, the town that serviced it had shrunk drastically, cut off as it was from the main El Paso road, isolated here in the high hills. Now only cattle and sheep kept it alive.

The bay snorted as Fargo tightened the cinch. Then he went to its head, started to unknot the reins looped around the hitch rack. At that moment, the two women came out of the store.

The Canfield women—in their sunbonnets and long dresses, their arms heaped high with purchases. Fargo watched them come down the steps, the old crone and the young girl, whose lithe swing of stride was visible even under the gingham that swathed her legs. He paused a moment in curiosity and admiration. Over her armload, her eyes met his again. Then —he never knew whether it was on purpose or accidental—she stumbled and the packages fell from her arms into the dusty street, almost at Fargo's boot toes.

"I swear, Bonnie, ye're clumsy as an ox." The old woman's voice was shrill.

"I'm sorry, Mama." The girl stooped, but Fargo had already bent to retrieve her packages. For a

20

moment, the two faces were very close together: the young, fresh, pretty one of Bonnie Canfield and the weathered, scarred, ugly one of Neal Fargo. In that instant, their eyes met, and the girl smiled, covertly, yet with boldness. "Thank you," she whispered.

"You're welcome," Fargo murmured, eyes still locked with hers. Then a big hand clamped on his shoulder, jerked him upright, spun him around. A hard fist slammed his jaw, literally picked him up with the blow's force, and dropped him in the dust. Shaking his head, trying to clear his eyes, he looked up at Jess Canfield, standing over him, the muzzle of the Henry rifle pointed at his belly.

"Stranger," the young man said, eyes blazing, "it's powerful bad medicine to mess with Canfield women."

"Don't be a fool, Jess!" Bonnie Canfield shouted. "He was just helpin' me with whut I dropped."

"Ye be quiet, sister. I seen what went on between ye two. All right, Mister. On yer feet, slow and easy and hand away from thet gun." He backed off a step or two.

The other Canfields had seen this. As, still covered by the young man's rifle, Fargo got warily to his knees, all those gunhung men came up and ringed around them. Roaring Tom pushed his way through the crowd as Fargo gained his feet. "All right," he snapped, planting himself between Fargo and his son. "Whut's a-happin' hyar?"

"He was lollygaggin' round Bonnie and she was teasin' him on like she always does. Was I you, I'd take a strap to her when we git home. Meanwhile, I figger on teachin' this ugly feller in the soldier hat to keep away from other folks' women."

Fargo was on his feet, now. There were too many gun-muzzles trained on him to risk a draw. He stood there, eyes shuttling from Canfield to his father.

"You got the wrong idea, fella," he said. "But you hit the wrong man, too. You want to lay down that Henry and show me how you can use that sixgun?"

"No guns!" Roaring Tom shook his fierce hawk's head. "I'll shoot the first man goes for his gun. Jess, ye knothead, ye're too damned sudden. Maybe the man didn't mean no harm."

"Back in the saloon, I seen him come outa the same room as Steed and Hanna," Jess said fiercely. "Anybody runs with them means harm to the Canfields." Suddenly he passed the Henry to the old man. "All right, Big Ugly. Pappy says no guns. But ye better be powerful good at knuckle and skull, because as soon as I git this side-gun off, I aim to come after ye and chop ye into stew beef." And his hand dropped to unlatch his gunbelt.

Chapter II

Overhead, a buzzard swirled on lazy wings. The wind sent dust sifting down the street; the sun was hot on Fargo's head, his hat knocked off by the force of Canfield's surprise blow. He stared into Jess's eyes for a moment, saw the mindless anger, the lust for violence in them. He knew he was not going to be able to leave this town without fighting Canfield. That was all right with him. His temper had been stretched to the last inch; now it snapped.

He smiled, a grin like that of a wolf sighting prey.

"All right, Canfield," he said quietly. His hand slid the belt tongue through the buckle. The holstered Colt made dead weight in his hand as he held it out to Roaring Tom. "You'll hold this for me and give it back when I've whipped him?"

"Ye whup him, ye'll git it back," Tom said. "You don't whup him, likely ye won't be in shape to need it. But if he's bound to fight ye, thet's his business." Then he turned to his son. "One thang. You fight

25

him, thet's the end of it. No matter which way it goes, it stops hyar, this ain't no fambly affair. If he whups you, don't look for nobody else to take up the quarrel."

Jess only laughed. "I don't need nobody else." He was stripping off his shirt, now, baring a torso bronzed and rippling with hard muscle. His biceps were enormous, bulging as he flexed his arms; his clenched hands looked like chunks of flint at the ends of thick wrists.

Now the ring of men gave way a little, spreading out. Fargo peeled away his own shirt. In this kind of fight, bare, sweaty skin was harder to seize and hold. A kind of murmur went up from the Canfields at the sight of his upper body. As bronzed and muscular as Jess's, less knotty and put together with more grace, it was scarred and blazed with old wounds of battle. Even Jess's eyes lit with a sort of admiration. "Feller, you been around."

"Yeah," Fargo said. He threw his shirt to Roaring Tom. It had no sooner left his hand than Jess charged.

Knuckle and skull: No holds barred, anything went. Fargo danced into a fighting crouch, but before he could get on balance, young Canfield hit him like an express train, clamped his arms around Fargo's body, bore him over and down by sheer weight and force. Fargo landed hard on the street, with Jess's solid weight on top of him, Canfield trying to get his knee in Fargo's groin, and his thumbs going for Fargo's eyes.

Fargo shielded himself with a practiced thigh from Jess's driving knee, and did not try to protect his eyes. Instead, he threw out his arms wide, like a man crucified, then brought them in again, fast and hard, palms open and turned. The tough edges of his hands bladed into Canfield's neck, one on either

26

side, with terrible impact. Canfield grunted, went momentarily lax. Fargo bucked, rolled, slid out from under. As he scrambled to his feet, Canfield lurched groggily up to his knees. He looked at Fargo, dazed eyes clearing, and his lips peeled back in a snarl. Before he could shove erect, though, Fargo moved in, caught him hard beneath the chin with a knee.

He heard the click of Canfield's teeth; blood ran out Jess's mouth from a bitten tongue. Jess flopped backward, and Fargo moved in to kick, stomp. It was the only way in a fight like this, the way Canfield fought.

But Jess was tough; even half unconscious, he reacted instinctively. Rolling away from Fargo's boot, he half somersaulted, came to his knees; then, as Fargo turned, was on his feet. He wasted not a minute, came in again, slugging this time with those huge fists. Fargo crouched again to meet the charge, sought an opening, but before he found one Jess landed a blow that would have killed a buffalo. It would have killed Fargo, too, if it had connected full and solid, but years in the prize ring had sharpened Fargo's every reflex. He rolled his head, swung his body. Jess's fist clipped his chin, slid off, slammed his shoulder. The blow sent Fargo spinning and Jess changed direction and came in once more and hit him in the belly before he could recover. All the breath went out of Fargo and then he was on the ground, gasping; and Jess's huge boot was blotting out the sun, about to crush his head.

Fargo caught that foot with both hands, exerting every ounce of steel-cable strength he possessed. And it took it to slow that hammering drive, stop the foot before it smashed his face. Then Fargo surged up, twisting, and Jess, off balance, staggered back. His foot slid out of Fargo's grasp, but as that happened, Fargo's grip pulled his boot half off. Jess jumped back, yanking at the straps, hobbling, and that gave Neal Fargo time to come up. The boot was still half on, half off, when he came at Jess.

This time he came in low, ready, on balance. Jess straightened up, raised his fists, trying to retreat and hampered by the boot. His guard, nevertheless, was surprisingly good; he and his brothers must have practiced. But it was not good enough; to a man with Fargo's trained eye and speed, Canfield's defense was full of holes. He lashed in with a short, hard flickering left, knuckles opening a slash on Canfield's cheekbone, whipping his head around. Fargo followed with another left, not driven more than six inches, but full of torque and power, and .caught the raw spot again. Jess grunted, raised his hands, and Fargo dropped and came in with a right that caught him on the breastbone. Before Jess recovered, Fargo hit him with a left again.

Jess staggered back, awkwardly, thrown off balance by the boot. Fargo came after him with cold precision. Canfield's huge fists whistled by his head as he drove Jess back with jabbing lefts and solid rights. Then, as he sensed Jess was getting wise to that pattern, mustering a defense against it, Fargo reversed it. What Canfield did not know was that he had been born ambidextrous, able to use right or left hand with equal facility and strength, able to balance his body from either side. He shifted weight and force completely, and Jess's new defense made no difference.

"Godamighty," some Canfield whispered. "He's cuttin' brother plumb to pieces! Pappy—"

Fargo hit Jess twice, right, left. Heard Roaring Tom's harsh command. "Lay down thet gun. This h'yar's Jess's ball of beeswax! The man's takin' him fa'r and squar'!"

"Damn ye," Jess Canfield breathed. His breath

rasped through a nose crushed and swollen, dribbling blood. His right eye was puffed almost shut; huge black bruises already made dark spots on his chest and belly. "Damn ye—" He backed, dragging the flopping boot, and Fargo kept on coming.

Now it was like chopping wood, hacking away at a huge tree that refused to fall. Fargo's fists, flicking past Jess's dazed and ever-widening guard, sounded, indeed, like an ax sinking into oak. Young Canfield's big head snapped back and forth, back and forth; and yet he would not go down. He hit back at Fargo, limply, without steam, but he refused to fall.

Fargo himself was panting, now, his wind almost gone, his knuckles bruised and bleeding. This had to be finished and finished soon. Suddenly he dropped his arms, let them dangle to his side. He stood there for a moment, breathing hard, sucking in great gulps of wind. Jess halted, blinking his one good eye in amazement at this sudden reprieve, the cessation of punishment. He shook his head wildly, to clear it, spraying blood from nose and mouth and chopped-up cheek. He raised his hands, braced himself to charge.

Then Fargo had the rest he needed. He came in cautiously, warily, and took his time. Jess started to lurch forward and Fargo saw the opening he wanted and made full use of it.

Every ounce of strength and muscle he possessed was behind that right, coming up from far down his body, gathering force with every inch it traveled, slamming finally into the exact point of Jess Canfield's jaw—the one place, hit hard enough, in which even the strongest man is vulnerable. Fargo felt the shock of impact all through his body. He stepped back. Jess stood there for an instant, hands falling, fists opening. His one good eye looked at Fargo strangely. Then all expression left it, and he fell

29

forward on his face with an impact that raised a cloud of dust.

Fargo stepped back farther, panting.

Jess Canfield lay motionless in the dirt. Only the bellows-pumping of his huge torso showed that he still lived.

From close by, Roaring Tom's voice came, trembling faintly. "Stranger, air ye gonna stomp him?"

Fargo wiped sweat and dust and blood from his own face. He sucked in air.

"Hit's your right, do whut ye choose to. He woulda done hit to ye." But fear for his son was plain now in Tom Canfield's tone.

Fargo looked at the old man through a mist of sweat. He licked dry lips. Roaring Tom stared back tensely. "I said thar'd be no interference. Thar won't be. Jess took his chances."

Fargo shook his head. "No," he said. "No, I ain't gonna stomp him."

There was a moment, then, when Roaring Tom looked incredulous. Then he sighed, and his shoulders slumped with relief. "I'm much obliged to ye fer thet. He's my baby boy."

"Your baby boy," Fargo mumbled and laughed shortly, rubbing his bruised face again. His eyes ached where Jess's thumbs had briefly pressed their sockets. "Yeah. All right. Well, you can have your baby boy. Just gimme my shirt and gun."

"They're yourn." Roaring Tom held the shirt, as Fargo slipped it on, passed back the Colt and gunbelt. "Mister, they're yourn." He looked into Fargo's face, and there was an intensity in his blue eyes. "Feller," he said harsely, "ye coulda stomped Jess plumb to death, and we woulda been bound not to raise a hand or pull a trigger. If it was ye layin there right now, Jess woulda pulped ye head. Them's the rules, and we stick by the rules." He hesitated. "I don't know whut yer name is—"

"Fargo. Neal Fargo."

"Mr. Fargo. I'll jest say this. There ain't many people welcome up whar we live in Black Valley. We don't take much to outsiders. But any time ye need a place to stay, a bit to eat, a drink of likker, or a gun to side ye, ye come to us, the Canfields."

Fargo looked at him in surprise.

"Thet's the way we air," said Roaring Tom. "I owe ye my son's life. Canfields always pay their debts."

Slowly, Fargo's mouth curled in a grin. He liked this old man, understood his code. "All right," he said. "If the time comes when I have to, I'll do that. But Black Valley ain't my range." He buttoned the shirt. "Likely I'll never see a Canfield again."

Then the girl was there, Bonnie. She held Fargo's old cavalry hat, the one issued to him in the Rough Riders. "This blowed off," she said.

"Thanks." Their eyes met again. This time, Fargo's shifted first. He wanted no more trouble with the Canfields, and what he saw in hers could easily have caused it.

He turned away, buckling on the gunbelt. Then, as Canfields made way for him, he went to the bay, swung tiredly into the saddle. He reined the horse around, looked at all those mountain men clustered in the street around the still unconscious Jess. As his eyes ranged over them, he grinned.

"Ye remember whut I said," Roaring Tom called earnestly.

"I'll remember," Fargo said. "But right now, I got business down on the Rio."

His hand went to the saddle scabbard on the left; the Winchester was still in place. In the one on the right, the sawed-off shotgun rode snugly. Satisfied, he swung the bay around, touched it with spurs, and loped out of Fort Davis. As he passed the saloon, he saw Steed and Hanna standing before it, staring at him with hostile, disappointed eyes. He did not even nod. It was a long way to El Paso and he had wasted too much time here already. Pancho Villa was waiting for ammunition; and Fargo needed money.

Once, at the edge of town, he twisted in the saddle, looked back. The Canfields were going to their horses. Only one remained in the center of the street, watching him: Bonnie. And as she raised her hand and waved, the old woman seized her and pulled her toward the wagon.

Fargo rode on, hard.

Chapter III

Two months later, on his second trip after leaving Fort Davis, the Texas Rangers ambushed him at the San Vicente crossing of the Rio, deep in the heart of the desolate Big Bend badlands.

He had come down to the river in the blackness of early morning—three o'clock—leading a string of half a dozen big and well-trained pack mules, each lugging four hundred pounds of ammunition for Pancho Villa. The normal load for a pack mule was two hundred, but Fargo had learned packing from a veteran of General Crook's expeditions against the Apaches years before, and he used the special saddles and pads Crook had devised to increase the loads an animal could carry. Right now, the more than ton of cartridges was worth a fortune in pure Chihuahua silver, and he was feeling good about having slipped past the Army so easily. Villa's spies along the river and his own sources of information kept him advised of Army movements and made it child's play to avoid the cavalry. But he had not counted on the Rangers being here, too. His first knowledge of their presence was when a voice, oddly familiar, blared from the brush along the river: "Halt! By order of the Texas Rangers!"

Fargo cursed. His double-barreled ten-gauge sawed-off shotgun rode muzzle downward across his shoulder in a sling. Instinctively, one hand went to it, then fell away.

In his long and dangerous life, he had broken nearly every manmade rule. But there was one he observed rigorously, a matter of self-preservation: *Never kill a Texas Ranger!*

He thought fast. Then he wheeled the bay so hard and suddenly it reared. He yanked the lead rope of the mules. They brayed in surprise, swung around. From the reeds along the river, gunfire roared. "Halt!" somebody yelled again. Flashes split the pitchblack darkness. Fargo bent low in the saddle as lead made its ugly whine around him. Then he and the mules were pounding up the slope, away from the Rio, headed for the shelter of the broken country. Behind him, he heard shouts, the thud of hooves.

Never kill a Texas Ranger!

The rule was becoming harder and harder not to break, Fargo thought bitterly, ten hours later. Penned up like a trapped cougar in this cave, his train of mules and their loads of ammo abandoned, taken by the Rangers, and now a half dozen of the lawmen down there, coming after him to smoke him out.

Thrusting the Winchester forward through the barricade of rocks that made a fort across the mouth of the shallow hole in this high wall of the Chisos Mountains, he let his finger caress the trigger. Break that rule, he told himself, shoot his way out—or

36

spend the next decade of his life in Huntsville or a Federal prison. When men came after him with guns, no matter who they were, he always fought back.

Below him on the steep, rock-strewn slope, the Rangers had fanned out. Each of the six had found good cover. They had recognized him by now and knew what he could do with the Winchester and the sawed-off shotgun. And they were in no hurry. They were six to one and they had food and water, and they could starve and thirst him out.

That was unless he made a break at nightfall. It was his only chance. With the Fox sawed-off, loaded nine buckshot to the barrel, he had a chance, a slim one, of blasting through when darkness covered him again. Meanwhile, if he were patient, likely he could reduce the odds with the carbine; one or two might get careless and give him a target before sundown came.

The fact remained, anyone who killed a Texas Ranger was doomed. Burn down one, much less two or three or six or however many he would have to drop before he fought free, and his death warrant was sealed. Once you killed a Ranger, the force would never rest until it killed you. Cross the Rio, flee beyond their jurisdiction, go to Canada or South America, it made no difference. Legally or otherwise, they would hunt you down. He knew himself to be as good a fighting man as any who ever burned powder. But not even he could stand against the Texas Rangers if he killed one of their number.

And so, squinting down at the sun-drenched slope, knowing they were there and waiting, he held his fire. One hand thumbed a thin cigar from the pocket of his sweat-drenched khaki shirt, thrust it between good, white teeth, then snapped a match and lit it. The smoke tasted fine and helped him think.

One thing he vowed: He would pull no time in prison.

In his violent career, he'd done everything but that. Born on a New Mexico ranch, orphaned before he could walk by a raiding party of Apaches, taken in by foster parents who had wanted not a child, but a slave, he had run away from his second home at the age of twelve. After that, all the things that Steed and Hanna had mentioned back there in Fort Davis. . . .

A soldier of fortune, he went where there was fighting to be done for money. And in all those rough years, he had spent no time in prison. Never had a warrant been sworn against him in the United States. But he had been cooped up temporarily in enough vile *carcels* south of the border to know that for a man who loved freedom and a high, wild, violent life as much as he did, five years or ten of prison would be worse than death. What he was faced with now was a choice between dying himself or killing Rangers; certainly he would not go to jail.

Below, now, the lawmen called to one another, but they could not see him. His wolf's grin spread across his face. Well, they'd not try to rush him until darkness; they were too wise for that. He had another hour to make up his mind what to do. The hell with it. He sat up, sliding back into the rock wall's shelter. Relax, enjoy the time he had left.

He took off the cavalry hat, ran his hand through the short, snow-white hair above the leather-colored, ugly face. There had to be some way, he thought, to get out of this, if he could only find it before his time ran out.

Meanwhile, he checked his weapons. The Winchester, a Model 94 carbine, was fully loaded; he laid it aside. The shotgun—his hands were gentler as he picked it up. A Fox Sterlingworth, it had once

38

been a fowling piece with long, full-choked barrels. But Fargo had sawed those off, leaving stubs with open bores, capable of throwing deadly scattering loads, converting it into the most lethal short-range weapon man had yet invented. His big hand caressed the ornate engraving on breech and barrels, worked out the legend traced there: *To Neal Fargo, gratefully, from T. Roosevelt.* His mouth twisted wryly. Well, that testimonial would not help him now.

He laid the Fox aside, drew the Colt .38 from its holster. It had been regular Army issue before the Army had gone to the Philippines. There, the unstoppability of the fanatical Moro tribesmen had made it seem inadequate, and the service had adopted the less accurate, less reliable, but heavier Colt .45 automatic. Fargo, however, clung to this weapon. He could stop anything that moved with it, Moro or not. The slugs in his cartridge belt were hollow-points, dum-dums that would fragment on impact, blowing a terrible wound in a man's flesh.

The main thing, he thought, was to hit where you aimed. Almost always, he did that.

The cylinder was fully loaded. He dropped it back into its scabbard. Then he drew the knife.

Not many people carried knives like this. He had got it in the Philippines, too. There they called it a Batangas knife, for the artisans in that province specialized in making these. Handles of water-buffalo horn, hinged, folded forward to cover most of a ten-inch blade of super-hardened steel. When, with his thumb, he flicked their catch and shook his wrist, they swung back together in his palm to make a grip. They revealed the long and deadly cutting edge and sharp point, hardened by a secret process. It could literally be driven through a silver dollar with a single blow without breaking or even dulling. He made the experienced knife-fighter's pass with his right hand, then shifted it to his left and repeated the maneuver, blade turned sideways, flat in relationship to the ground. His hand was like a snake's strike, blurred and swift.

Then he returned the Batangas knife to its sheath. He checked his cartridge bandoliers. He had spent some Winchester ammo in the running fight, firing over the heads of the pursuing Rangers in a fruitless attempt to slow them down. But he had not used the shotgun, and the bandolier that held fifty rounds for it was still full. He adjusted them crisscross over his chest; their weight was somehow comforting.

Still, what he had to decide was whether to die or kill some Rangers. And time was growing short; outside, the sun was dropping, shadows lengthening.

He edged back to the mouth of the cave, sprawled his long, khaki-clad body behind the rocks again and thrust the carbine forward once more. The Rangers were still under cover.

No jail, he decided firmly. Whatever happened, no jail. What was it the old Cheyennes had said when they went into battle?

This is a good day to die.

He crushed out his last cigar and waited.

Then the voice rang up the slope, calling his name.

"Fargo," it bawled. "Hey, Neal!"

Fargo stiffened.

"Neal Fargo! This is Mart Penny callin' to you!"

Fargo swore softly. The Rangers had been too far behind for him to recognize them. But now he knew why that voice blaring from the river brush had seemed to familiar.

Fargo's mind flashed back. Once, in Cuba, he and Mart, just the two of them, had stood off a whole platoon of Spaniards until Bucky O'Neill's company could come up. This made it even trickier. He licked dry lips. "Mart!" he bellowed. "What the hell you doin' down there?"

"What the hell you think? I'm captain of this Ranger company!"

"Well, that's your tough luck!" Fargo yelled back.

"Neal, don't be a fool! I want to talk to you!"

"About what? Huntsville? Leavenworth?"

"Maybe, maybe not!" Penny's voice echoed off the barren rock of the mountainside. "Will you parley with me?"

"About what? Surrender? Spend the rest of my life inside the goddamn walls? You go to hell!"

"Neal, you ain't got a chance! Don't you see that?"

"I got my guns!"

"Makes no difference! Kill us, kill us all, every Ranger in Texas will be on your tail. Neal, damn it, talk to me!"

Fargo hesitated. "You want to come up all alone, flag of truce?"

"Hell, I'll shuck my guns, come up slick."

"What is it you want to talk about?"

"Can't yell it. Plumb private! Let me come up!"

Fargo gnawed his lower lip. Then he made his decision. "All right, Mart. You come up slick, hands above your head. No tricks, though. Any tricks, old times don't mean a thing."

"You think I don't know that? Fargo, I'm standin' up. You can see me shuck my guns."

"Go ahead," Fargo called. "You're safe as in church."

His narrowed eyes swept the slope. There were boulders down there big as houses. Then something edged around one: In the slanting light and purple shadows, it resolved into the figure of a man, tall, wide in the shoulders, narrow in the hips, wearing a big black sombrero, a Ranger "scout belt" containing loops for rifle and pistol cartridges alike, a gray flannel shirt and batwing chaps that blended neatly with the background, and a silver star inside a circle on his left breast that made a superb target.

Fargo watched him unlatch the scout belt, let it drop. With it went his sixgun. Then Penny raised his hands above his head, and under the aim of Fargo's gun, began the long walk up the slope.

As the Ranger captain neared, Fargo saw that he'd not changed much. The same crinkled eyes, the snub nose, the wide mouth and jutting, rocklike chin: Beneath his high-heeled boots, gravel slipped and rolled as he panted up the slope, hands high. Then he was at the cave's mouth.

"Stop right there, Mart," said Fargo. "I want to look you over."

"No hideout, Neal. Even left my knife."

Fargo's eyes detected no suspicious bulge. Damn it, even like this, it was good to see Mart Penny again. When had been the last time? San Antonio, about 1905? Mart hadn't been a Ranger then, and it had been one hell of a drunk they'd tossed together and a lot of saloons they'd torn apart.

"Okay, you damned lawdog," he said. "Come on in."

Penny grinned. "Comin', hardcase." He bent, stepped over the rock barrier, edged inside as Fargo shoved back, Winchester still trained.

Penny looked around. "Not much on comfort, Neal."

"I was aimin' to write the landlord a letter," Fargo said. "Sit down, Mart."

"Yeah. The shade feels good. Must be a hundred out there in that sun." Penny dropped, leaned against the wall, panting slightly from the climb. He was the same age as Fargo and his beard, unshaved

42

during this patrol, was faintly tinged with gray. He took off his hat, fanned his face. "Neal, how you been?"

"Better than I am now, Mart."

"Likely. You won't plug me if I light a cigarette?"

"Not if you give me one. Just smoked my last cigar."

The Ranger took out a pack of Sweet Caporals, passed Fargo one, lit one himself. "Well, he said, pluming smoke through both nostrils, "we come a long way, Neal."

"If I'd known you were gonna join the Rangers, I'd have let that Mexican go ahead and cut you when he found you in the hay with his *señorita*, back in San Antone."

"Lord God, I'd forgotten that!" They looked at one another, grinning. Then Penny's face was serious. "Neal, you're in a fix."

"I figured that out all by myself."

"If you don't surrender, we'll have to kill you."

"If I do, I'll go to prison. I don't like prisons, Mart."

"You shouldn'ta violated that embargo. No arms to Villa; you know that."

"It used to be all right."

"Before President Wilson changed his policy."

"Somebody in Washington signs a paper. Then for what's been legal, they can pen you up the rest of your life."

"I don't like it any better than you. Villa's the only decent fighting man those poor bastards down there have got on their side. All the same, law's law and orders are orders. And I'm sworn to enforce the one and follow the other. No more guns or ammo to the Mes'cans."

"Yeah. I hope you didn't come all the way up that

hill to tell me that. Nor to ask me to surrender, either. Because you know I won't."

"I ain't that much fool. But Neal, there is a chance."

Fargo stared at him. "What kind of chance?"

"To leave here on your feet and with your guns. Kill no Rangers and never see the inside of a prison."

"Mart, the sun ain't got to you?" Fargo drew in a breath of smoke. "You aim to let me go?"

"I didn't say that," Penny answered. "I want to make a trade."

"What kind of trade?"

"Your life, guns, and freedom," Penny said. "In return for doing me a favor."

"What kind of favor?"

"I've got a warrant on a man. I want it served. I want you to serve it and bring that man in."

"Me?" Fargo's voice was astonished. "What man?"

Penny's eyes were hard. "His name's Jess Canfield," he said. "We want him dead or alive. But, given a choice, we'd rather have him dead. Three weeks ago he killed a Texas Ranger."

For a moment, there was total silence in the cave. Down the slope a mule, one of Fargo's brayed.

"Do you know about the Canfields?" Penny asked.

"I know about them."

"All right. A month ago, two riders working for a man named Steed followed some strays to their hole-in-the-wall up yonder in the Davis Mountains. Somebody bushwhacked 'em outside that gorge called Black Canyon. Killed one of the men; the other got out with a shoulder wound. He got a look at the guy who drygulched 'em, identified him as

Jess Canfield. Walt Steed swore out a warrant against Canfield for murder."

His mouth twisted in contempt. "The local sheriff wouldn't serve it. Flat out refused to, said he wasn't gittin' mixed up with the Canfields. Said he'd never be able to bring Jess in without killin' him, and if he did that, he'd have all the other Canfields after him and his life wouldn't be worth a nickel. So he hollered for the Rangers."

Penny looked toward the Rio. "We'd jest received orders to move our whole company down here to patrol the border. I couldn't spare but one man—my best. I sent Bat Carson up there to serve the warrant. Moved the rest of the company down here. Word reached me through the Army weeks ago that some of Steed's men found Bat dead outside of Black Canyon. He had been shot in the back with .44 rifle bullets; looked to the sheriff like loads for a Henry. I understand Jess Canfield carries a .44 Henry."

"He does," Fargo said.

Penny's lean, beardy face was grim. "There is nothin' I'd like better," he said harshly, "than to take my whole company up there and wipe out that nest of hillbilly snakes, beginnin' with Jess Canfield. But Austin won't let me. They say I got to keep every man down here on the Rio until further notice. Meanwhile—well, Bat Carson was a man I have rode on many a scout with. Savin' maybe you, I never had a better friend."

"I'm beginnin' to see," said Fargo.

"Austin says they'll send a man, some men, soon, when they've got some free. I don't feel like waiting. I want Canfield's hide and I want it now. I want you to get it for me."

"I'm no law officer," Fargo said.

"No. But you ain't no outlaw, either, unless I

45

bring you in this go-round. And—I've got another warrant for Jess Canfield down yonder in my saddlebags. With it in your possession, you could go up yonder and make a citizen's arrest of Canfield."

Fargo ground out his cigarette. He shook his head, trying to analyze this proposition. Never had he run into anything like this before.

"He wouldn't come without some lead in him," he said at last.

"That's what I'm hopin'," Penny said.

His voice roughened. "Don't think the Rangers are gettin' too weak to kill their own snakes. If I could get loose, I'd like nothin' better than to go up there and brace Canfield myself. I know I could take him. The only other man I know who could is you."

Fargo was silent. Presently he said, "Has it occurred to you that if I killed Jess Canfield I'd have his whole family down on me? They'd declare a blood feud against me. From Roarin' Tom on down to the youngest kid that could sight a rifle. They wouldn't rest until they got me. The only way I could save myself would be to kill them all."

Penny looked straight into his eyes, without expression. "As long as it was in self-defense—"

"That's what you want me to do, isn't it?" Fargo said quietly.

"Let's look at it this way," Penny said. "Canfield's killed a Ranger. That means a Ranger has got to kill Canfield. That means the other Canfields will declare war against the Rangers. It means that the Rangers will have to wipe them out sooner or later. And it means some Rangers will get killed doing it, because we can only operate in a certain way; we can't shoot until fired upon. It will be a blood feud between the Canfields and the Rangers, and will go on and on. But not if somebody else kills Canfield. A private citizen, somebody who's not a Ranger.

46

You, Neal. I want Jess Canfield either brought in for trial or dead. What happens after that won't concern us—unless somebody swears out a warrant against you. And the Canfields never went to the law in their whole life."

He paused. "I'd never make anybody but you such a proposition. But it's no wilder than some of the jobs you've done for Teddy Roosevelt on the sly. That revolution in Panama that gave him the excuse to send in Marines and secure the Canal Zone so he could dig the Big Ditch. A few other jobs I've heard rumors of. More than once, you've pulled off some deals nobody else could have done."

"For money," Fargo said.

"I can't pay you any money," Penny said. He looked out the cave, down the slope to where the other Rangers waited in concealment. "All I can offer you is your life and freedom."

"I take this job, my life ain't likely to be long."

"It'll be even shorter if you don't." Penny's voice was cold. "God knows, Neal, after what we've been through together, I don't want to have to kill you. But if we don't make a deal right now, you've only got two choices. Come out with your hands up and go to prison, or come a-shooting. And you can't burn down us all—not even with that arsenal. I'm at least offering you a chance to see another sunrise."

Fargo said, "Let me have another cigarette. I think better when I'm smokin'."

"Take the pack. I got more down there."

Fargo lit the cigarette.

"You say yes," Penny went on, "give me your word that you'll go after Jess Canfield and serve that warrant, I wouldn't be surprised if, when dark comes, you couldn't make it down that slope without nobody seein' you. Wouldn't surprise me if you found a saddled horse down there behind that big boulder that looks like the crown of a hat. And, prob'ly, that warrant for Canfield would be in the saddlebags. Damned if it ain't likely you'd get clean away. And we'd never even know whose ammo it was we confiscated."

"Yeah," Fargo said.

"So?"

"Thirty mountain men or six Rangers." Fargo's voice was wry. He smoked a moment longer. Then he made up his mind. "All right, Mart. I'll take the thirty mountain men."

Penny's voice was full of relief. "Your hand on it?"

"Here." And Fargo put it out.

Penny looked at him silently for a second or two, released it, stood up.

"After dark, Neal," he said. He went to the cave's mouth, halted, turned. "Bring me Canfield's scalp." He smiled faintly. "So long, hardcase."

"*Adios*, lawdog," Fargo said, and watched him go down the slope and vanish behind a boulder.

He crushed out the cigarette. This was not a deal he liked at all. But he had no choice. Then he grinned, slowly, coldly. So he would have to fight the whole Canfield clan after all. Well, that being the case, there was no reason why he should not make twenty thousand dollars on the side for doing it.

Chapter IV

There was food in the saddlebags and water in the canteen slung across the horn; and the horse was a good one. Fargo made it down the slope without a shot being fired, swung up into the saddle. He socked home spurs. Then, as he galloped out from behind the hat-shaped rock, bent low, gunfire ripped the desert silence. Lead whined high above him. Mart Penny could say in his report that the arms-runner had escaped under heavy fire and be truthful.

He rode all night, taking a circuitous route through the badlands of Big Bend, which he knew like the back of his own scarred hand. Morning found him west and north of Study Butte, holed up in a deep arroyo. He had slept four hours, the shotgun cradled in his arm, awakened, and was eating a few bites of jerky when the horse, hobbled, snorted and pricked its ears. Fargo caught that warning at once. With the shotgun slung across his shoulders, its muzzles down his back, he went silently up the dry stream bed's wall.

The three horsemen had but his trail, were working across the flat out there toward the arroyo. He squinted into the morning light; then he relaxed. They were neither cavalry nor Rangers: They wore straw sombreros and loose white shirts crisscrossed with cartridge-laden bandoliers, ragged pants and high black boots. Mexicans. Not part of Villa's band this far north of the Rio. His lips thinned. No, they would be some of Chico Cana's bandits.

Fargo's eyes glittered; his teeth gleamed as his mouth warped into a sort of snarl. Cana was a vulture, operating around Presidio: rustler, hold-up artist, he and his sizeable gang preyed on anybody who had a dollar or a gun or a horse or a watch, even their own people, the Mexican-Americans. These three *bandidos* probably counted themselves fortunate in having struck the trail of a lone horseman. Three against one; they'd have no trouble in rubbing him out, taking his mount, his saddle, any other goods he might have. Likely they were counting on even stripping the boots from his corpse.

Fargo slid back down the bank of the arroyo. He checked the horse's hobbles. He laid his own Winchester and his unstrapped Colt across his saddle, along with the canteen. Then he went quickly up the arroyo to where, fifty yards from all that gear he had put out as bait, it turned. Behind the bend, he hunkered against the bank, sheltered by an overhang. Then, patiently as any coyote outside a chicken coop, he waited.

He heard them enter the arroyo through the same sloping notch that he had used. Their voices carried a long way in the desert air, and, very confident, they did not keep them down.

"It is not an Anglo soldier," one said. "The shoes of the horse are not the Army type."

"More likely it is a messenger from the Mariscal

Mine, or the one at Study Butte. If we are very lucky, perhaps he carries a payroll."

"*Ay, Dios!* No use to count on luck like that. But he'll have a horse and some guns we can use—and if we bring back nothing from this sweep, Chico will be very unhappy."

Then one said, "Hush. No use to announce our coming."

They fell silent. Fargo's horse snorted, nickered a greeting. Another horse returned it. Fargo tensed. They would just about be now at the place where he had made camp.

"*Valgame Dios!*" One of them laughed. "He has heard us coming and has fled. Leaving us this good horse, saddle, guns, all. Yanqui chicken-heart. Well, he can't go far on foot. Juan, you keep an eye open. We'll saddle the horse and lead it. Then we'll run him down."

That was when Fargo stepped around the corner of the bank.

In Spanish, he said: "That won't be necessary."

The three were dismounted, gathered around the saddle and the guns. They whirled, reaching for their pistols, eyes wide with surprise.

Fargo's mouth had time to curl in contempt for such greedy amateurs as his right hand went up, thumb hooking in the shotgun's sling. That thumb twitched; the short twin barrels jerked up beneath his arm, pointing forward, although upside down. His left hand flashed across his body, tripped both triggers in a smooth, flawless gesture.

It had worked perfectly: His bait had gathered them into a tight knot around the saddle and the guns. Now, eighteen buckshot went hosing down the arroyo, spreading at thirty yards, in a pattern wide enough to chip them down like wheat before a scythe. That leaden hail slammed into three bodies

53

with tremendous force. One of them just had time to fire a shot from his drawn Colt; it plowed uselessly into the sand of the arroyo wall. It was the only shot any of them fired. Two were slammed backward by the chopping impact of the heavy pellets; the third was knocked to one side with slugs in the right arm and shoulder and fell across Fargo's saddle blanket. He kicked and twisted, trying to reach his Colt with his left hand, his face contorted, eyes wide and staring. But Fargo had already unslung the Fox. It opened, flicking empties, and his thumb had punched another round from the bandolier across his chest. It went in instantly; a snap of his wrist closed the gun and he pulled the right trigger and the full force of nine shot sent the last man rolling off the blanket and across the sand, where, chopped horribly by all that lead, he lay still.

Fargo broke the gun again, punched in two more rounds. With it at the ready, he went down the arroyo. But there was no need this time for his habitual caution. The three of them were dead.

Fargo picked up his Colt, strapped it on. Their horses, at the gun-thunder, had fled down the draw. His own hobbled, snorted and curveted, wild-eyed. Fargo bridled it, mounted it bareback, rode down the draw until he caught up with the mounts of the Mexicans. He sized them up; two sorry nags, a mixture of cold blood and mustang, and one damned good sorrel with pure Spanish blood, stolen from some hacienda. He caught the sorrel. When he put the bridle from Mart Penny's horse on it, he saw its mouth was raw and tender from a spade bit to which a piece of barbed wire had been added. He cursed its dead owner with the ferocity of a born horseman.

When it was bridled, he let Mart Penny's horse go; he did not want to be caught crossing Texas on an animal with a Ranger brand. He put his own saddle and saddlebags on the sorrel, seated the Winchester in its boot, decided to keep the shotgun slung. He mounted up, rode north and west again. A half hour later, he stopped and twisted in the saddle, looking back, a dozen vultures circling in the bright blue bowl of sky.

Fargo made good time; three nights later, he drew rein outside an adobe hut on the outskirts of Marfa. It was past twelve, and no lights burned here in the Mexican quarter on the cowtown's south side. But a small dog roused itself, yapped around the sorrel's feet until the animal kicked it and sent it ki-yiing off. Then the hut's wooden door swung open cautiously, and, limned by the lamplight inside, Nina Alvarez stood silhouetted there.

She was thirty, childless, her husband had crossed the Rio to join Villa and had been killed in Durango. So far as the Anglos here in Marfa were concerned, she was just another Mexican washerwoman. Actually, she was one of Villa's best spies north of the Rio and an indispensable link in the apparatus for running guns and ammo that Fargo had set up with the guerrilla leader.

She wore a thin cotton nightgown, and the light shone through it and outlined every curve of a full-breasted, slim-waisted, wide-hipped, short-legged body. "*Quien es?*" she called softly; and then, as he swung down, she recognized him. "Neal!"

When he entered the hut, closing the door behind him, she ran into his arms, pressing the soft pillows of her breasts against him, greedily opening her mouth for his kiss. He held her for a while. When they parted, she said: "You got the bullets to Pancho safely?"

"No," said Fargo.

"What?" Her eyes widened.

"Fix me a bath and some food. I'll tell you later. Now I'll see to the horse."

He fed the horse and watered it and left it in the little stable, still saddled and hackamored, so if he needed it in a hurry, it would be ready. When he went back into the hut and unslung all his guns, Nina kissed him again. She had a tub of warm water waiting, a bottle of tequila on the table, frijoles and tortillas cooking. Fargo went directly to the bottle, drank long and thirstily, and sighed.

"Now," she said. "Tell me what happened."

As he undressed, he told her, omitting his deal with Penny. "Pancho will have to bring in more weapons through Nogales. The Rangers have got the Texas border sealed off tight."

"Then I will pass the word to him." When he was seated, luxuriously, in the tub, she washed his back. From time to time, he dragged on the bottle. Presently she came with food; he ate that, too, while he soaked.

"Will you try a load through Nogales?" she asked.

"Later. I've got something else to do right now. Joe Morrison in Phoenix will have to increase his volume." He splashed out of the tub, dried with the towel she handed him. By the time he'd finished, she had slipped off the thin nightgown and lay on the cot, waiting for him. Before he went to her, he moved his Colt and shotgun within easy reach of the bed. Then he lowered himself onto her softness.

Walt Steed branded *Lazy S*. For miles before he reached the Davis Mountains, Fargo had seen pastures full of fat whiteface cattle with that iron burned on their hips. Now that the war in Europe had reached a peak of fury, cattle were worth their weight in gold, and the rich grama of the basins and valleys of that hill country would put poundage on them miraculously fast. That was why Steed and Hanna had been willing to pay through the nose to get their hands on the vast acreage of Black Valley graze again. Fargo hoped they still were.

It was nearly sunset when he turned off up the lane that led to the Lazy S headquarters. When it came in sight, nestled at the foot of a juniper-clad peak, its multiple windmills spinning in the evening breeze, he drew rein, sucked in a breath of sheer appreciation. It had been a long time since he had seen a layout like that. Black Valley range or no, Steed was well on his way to becoming a cattle king of a magnitude rivaling that of such historic figures as Charles Goodnight and John Chisum.

Ahead, a big frame house of sawn lumber, freshly painted, gleamed in the slanting light. Around it was a vast complex of bunkhouses, cookshacks and corrals. Fargo, holding the sorrel tight-gathered, tipped back his hat. Steed would have a lot of riders, of course. But it seemed to him that there were more men lounging around the ranch yard than called for even on a spread of this size. Then the sorrel snorted as a volley of gunshots sounded, like firecrackers at this distance.

The men around the corrals and bunkhouses paid no attention. The shots came again, and now Fargo had pinpointed their source. On the slope behind the house, more than a dozen men were taking target practice. And, Fargo thought, the way they were burning ammunition, someone else was paying for it. His mouth thinned; he touched the sorrel with spurs and sent it loping down the lane.

As he drummed into the yard, the lounging men looked curiously at the newcomer in the battered cavalry hat, the double-barreled sawed-off riding muzzles down behind his shoulder. In turn, as Fargo reined in, he appraised them. Some of them were ordinary cowhands, all right. But, standing out among them like wolves in a flock of sheep, there were gunmen, fighting men. Unlike the punchers, they wore holstered sixguns or Colt automatics. Lean and hardfaced, they began to sift together in a tight knot, forming a kind of pack in case this man, whom they recognized as one of their kind, meant trouble. Up on the hill, another volley of gunfire sounded.

Fargo rubbed his chin thoughtfully. Walt Steed was in the process of putting together an army. And that could mean only one thing. Rangers and soldiers be damned; he had made up his mind to go into Black Valley and take it back by force.

Which, Fargo thought, halting before the big ranch house, might make it tricky to deal with Steed.

He swung down, tethered the sorrel, strode up on the big house's wide veranda, knocked on the door.

There was a space of time before anyone answered, and during that interval, Fargo's eyes swept the ranch yard again. The gunmen—he counted them, plus that group up on the hill—stood quietly, ranked in front of a corral fence, watching him impassively. Then he heard booted feet inside. The door opened and, as Fargo turned, Steed himself was there.

His small blue eyes widened in surprise as he recognized his caller. Then his mouth twisted almost contemptuously. "So you came back," he said.

"That's right," Fargo said.

"You got hungry after all."

"Let's just say things have changed. I'm ready to deal with you and Hanna, now. If you still want that job done."

"You're too late," Steed said. "I decided to do it myself." His eyes went to the bunch of gunmen over by the corral. "I can use another man, though. I'm payin' two hundred a month for top guns."

58

Fargo took out cigarettes, thrust one in his mouth. "You're buyin' a lot a trouble for yourself tryin' it this way."

"Maybe, maybe not. All the Rangers and the Army's gone south to play games with Villa. That leaves me a clear field. When I git through with Black Valley, there won't be a Canfield left alive in there. Once I'm on the ground and holdin' it, let's see anybody throw me out. Well? You want a job?"

"Not that kind," Fargo said.

Steed spat past him into the dust. "Then ride on," he said.

Fargo did not move. "It'll take fifty men to do that job."

"I'll have fifty men."

"That's ten thousand a month. Might take you two months. Plus the law you'll have to deal with later. You'll be out twenty-five thousand, easy. You and Hanna together, paying me, you're only on the hook for ten."

"Hanna ain't in this," Steed said. "It's been three months since we talked to you. Things have changed. Hanna used to be the big dog up here, but when I get Black Valley, he won't be no more. And there ain't going to be no trouble with the law. I got the sheriff in my pocket. He'll back me up on anything I say. While the Rangers and the Army's gone, the time's hot to strike. I'm askin' you one more time. You want to hire on for wages?"

"I don't work for wages," Fargo said.

"Then ride on," Steed said again.

Fargo looked at him for a moment. "All right," he said at last, "I reckon I'll do that." He turned away, went down the steps.

Then a voice called his name. "Fargo! Hey, Neal!"

He whirled. Stared. Slowly his mouth split in its wolf's grin. "Gordon! Lin Gordon!"

The man who had come around the ranch house at the head of the group that had been shooting on the hill was tall, gaunt, cadaverous, with sunken cheeks and deepset eyes and a huge blade of a nose. He wore two Colt .45's, their gunbelts crisscrossed over his flat belly. His smile was cool, revealing big yellow teeth. "Hell," he said, "I ain't seen you since we worked together up yonder in Oklahoma. What you doin' down here?"

Fargo's mind flashed back to the oil fields where he and Gordon and Gordon's wild bunch, the gunmen who acknowledged him as leader and fought wherever he hired them out, had helped bring in a vast new oil field. "I might ask you the same question. I thought your cut of those wells up in Golconda would have put you on easy street."

"Same goes for you."

"I got restless," Fargo said. "Sold out my share. Managed to spend an awful lot of money awful fast. Had to go back to working for a living."

"Same with us. Too much money makes an *hombre* soft." Gordon glanced back over his shoulder at the dozen hardcases behind him. "We sold out, too. It don't take long for it to go, does it?"

"No," Fargo said. "So now you and your bunch are workin' for Steed?"

"That's right. Understand we're to clean out a bunch of hillbillies up yonder in the mountains. You comin' in with us?"

"No," Fargo said.

Even the cold smile vanished, then. "You're not gonna be against us, are you?"

"I don't know yet," Fargo said.

Gordon stood there a moment, hands dropping loosely to his hips. "Now, Neal, you know better than that. You don't want to get crosswise of us. I mean, you're good. Dammed good. But when it comes down right to the bone—"

"You're thinking you're a little better."

"Well, that just might be possible. There ain't many of us left. Not much for a man to sharpen his teeth on any more."

"Don't try to sharpen 'em on me, Lin."

"I don't aim to. Unless you git where we might stumble over you. I'm ramroddin' this fightin' operation for Steed. You want to come in as my second in command—"

"You know me better than that," said Fargo.

"Yeah. You don't like to be second in nothing, do you?"

"A man that's satisfied with second don't live long in this business."

Gordon grinned. "Ain't that the truth?" The grin went away. "Neal, you plannin' to stay up in this country?"

"Maybe. For a spell."

"Then jest stand clear. Don't git underfoot."

"That's a warning?"

"That's a warning," Gordon said.

"We'll see what happens," Fargo said. He went to the sorrel, unlatched its reins from the hitchrack. "Steed told me to ride. I reckon I'd better ride. See you around, Lin."

"Yeah," Gordon said.

Fargo mounted lithely. Gordon watched him as he spurred out of the yard. Fargo kept the horse moving fast down the lane, and from time to time glanced over his shoulder. Gordon was right; there were not many of them left nowadays; not north of the Rio, anyhow. And of those who were, Neal Fargo and Lin Gordon were the cream of the crop. Somehow such men were drawn to one another like magnets. Often they worked together; just as often, they wound up on opposite sides. Either way, it made no difference. The main thing was the fighting; the need to go up against someone worthy of their steel. Gordon was feeling that need, now; the itch to match himself against Neal Fargo, prove that he was better.

Maybe he was, Fargo thought. There was this hard knowledge in him: that someday he was indeed bound to run up against a better man. Age and old wounds slowed a gunfighter. He could not stay on top forever. Sooner or later he had either to get out of the business or take the inevitable bullet thrown by somebody a little younger, or who had taken less damage in other battles, or who drank a little less and kept his reflexes quicker. Or maybe who, on that particular day, when it came, was just luckier.

Given a choice, Fargo would take the bullet over retirement. He had no desire to grow old and feeble and feel himself coming apart bit by bit and piece by piece, wind up his days helpless in a rocking chair. Nor did he want to be left behind by time. Someday he would be obsolete in a world where there was no place for men who lived as he did—wild, free, by their wits and skill as fighters. Someday the world would be settled, quiet, overrun with law and civilization; and there would be no more place for him—or for Lin Gordon, either—in such a world than there would be for a timber wolf in farming country. Meanwhile, though, he would live as he always had, pushing every minute to its limit, wholly, totally alive. Somewhere even now the bullet with his name on it might have already been cast, was riding in someone's cartridge loop—Gordon's, or a Mexican soldier's, or a Canfield's. Until then, he would take his women where he found them, his whiskey when he was thirsty, and his chances as they came.

He reined in, looked back again. Gordon had challenged him. As sure as chalk was white, sooner or later, somewhere, whether in Texas or South America or some place he had not even been yet or dreamed of, he would have to meet that challenge. He felt a kind of savage pleasure in that knowledge, the same sort Gordon must have felt. Then he tensed, rose in his stirrups.

Back there in the yard, Gordon and Steed were standing close together, talking. He could see Steed half-gesture toward himself, Gordon nod. Fargo let his mouth curl in its wolf's grin again. Then he rode on, fast.

It was a long way to Hanna's ranch. He camped that night at Point of Rocks on the old Overland Stage Trail. Here a huge jumble of house-sized boulders towered above the west side of the Fort Davis road. Beyond stretched a range of peaks, juniper-clad and scabbed with raw rock outcroppings.

He picketed the sorrel on the east side of the road where the grass was lush. On the west, just below the huge rock face, he put down his saddle beneath big oaks, spread his blankets and built a fire. He ate slab bacon and a can of beans, washed it down with water and a few jolts of tequila from a bottle in his saddle bags. He leaned his shotgun against the saddle and then gathered some rocks. He laid these on his blanket and put another blanket over them, then backed off and surveyed the effect in the flickering firelight. He would have liked to take the shotgun up the hillside with him, but he knew that Gordon would have warned his men about it and they would be reassured by the sight of it near his bed. Because it was cold in these mountains at night, he donned a sheepskin jacket. Then he climbed up among the boulders that towered for a hundred feet over his bed, found a niche halfway up in which he could be comfortable, and sank down to rest and wait. While he did so, he checked the cartridges in the Winchester and spun the cylinder of the .38, making sure it was in order and fully loaded.

He thought he had it figured out now. If he were wrong, the most he could lose was a night's comfortable sleep. If he were right, he was saving his life.

Darkness deepened. He had made a big fire and it burned for a long time. By ten o'clock it still flickered, reduced to a bed of coals with occasional bursts of flame. Coyotes were yapping now, and occasionally a cow bawled. Fargo had taken the tequila up into his rock stronghold with him, and he nipped from the bottle from time to time as he waited. He wondered if Gordon would come himself or only send a detail. He rather thought the latter. There were subtle reasons for thinking so, not the least of which was Gordon's hope that he might escape, survive, to give Gordon the pleasure of meeting him face to face.

Fargo waited. He thought about the Mexicans, Chico Cana's men. Maybe he was pushing his luck, using essentially the same trap twice in ten days. Maybe Gordon's wild bunch was smarter than the Mexicans. Maybe—

Then he came alert. Sound traveled a long way in this air on such a night. They should have reined in, dismounted, a long way back. But they had not; and that meant that Gordon was not with them. And because they would rather ride than walk, were too lazy to take the necessary pains to make sure of their prey. He grinned, and his hand closed around the Colt's grip. Gordon must be testing some of the hired gunmen who were not part of his own bunch.

Then they did dismount; he no longer caught the thud of hoofbeats. Minutes passed with molasses slowness, stringing out in a way that would have been intolerable to an untrained fighting man. But patience was as much Fargo's stock in trade as the specially loaded cartridges in the revolver. He did not move a muscle.

Presently he saw them: four of them. They had spotted the fire and were advancing on foot in a kind of skirmish line. The moon was up just enough to silhouette their figures, glint a little on the barrels of the rifles they carried. He supposed there was one more somewhere further back; a horseholder.

They came forward up the road, spread out ten feet apart, crouched, slinking toward the fire. Say this for them, he thought: They made no sound. At least they'd had sense enough to take off their spurs and lever rounds in their rifles before they approached, so no telltale snick of loading would give them away.

Behind the fire, the humped bedroll full of rocks made an easy target. They came on, sure that they were approaching a man sleeping after a hard day's travel. When they were close enough to see the shotgun leaning against the saddle, two of them fell back, and two moved forward, bent low, Indian style.

Now they were very near the fire; they wanted to be absolutely certain. Ten yards away from the heap of glowing coals, the pair halted. Fargo changed weapons from necessity, laid aside the Colt, putting it on a rock within easy reach, picked up the already loaded Winchester.

The two closest to the fire lined their rifles, prepared to saturate the bedroll with lead. Fargo

65

grinned and pointed his own Winchester at the other two farther off. He pulled the trigger. The wham of the gun was startlingly loud in the tense silence. A man screamed, fell kicking. Fargo jerked in another round, shot again, and the second man went down before he even had time to yell in surprise. Then Fargo seized the Colt.

The men near the fire were in easy range and excellent targets as they stood frozen in surprise. Fargo fired the revolver once and the gunman on the right, hit by the hollow-point, was jerked off his feet, sent spinning backwards. The fragmenting bullet inside his chest cut off his life before he could cry out. The other, catching the gun flash, raised his Winchester with a single surprised oath. Fargo had intended to hit him in the torso, but the man got off a round and lead whined against the rock behind which Fargo was sheltered; and that threw off his aim a bit. The .38 slug caught the gunman in the head. His skull exploded, and his body fell forward across the fire, shirt bursting into flames.

Fargo picked up the Winchester, moved soundlessly down the rock face. He began to run. He ran silently and fast, in the direction from which the quartet had come, staying well away from the edge of the winding road. Then he heard a horse's snort, slowed. A man called out: "Bruce. Hey, Bruce—"

Fargo saw the crown of a hat silhouetted against the moonlit sky; five horses skittering nervously as its wearer held their reins with one hand, dragging his sixgun with the other, Fargo lined the Winchester, fired. The horses, free, whirled and went galloping off into darkness.

And that was all of them. Fargo ran back up the road. His own sorrel was snorting at the end of its picket rope. He uncuffed its hobbles, pulled its picket pin. In moments, he had it saddled, all his gear loaded. He swung up, lashed it with the reins. It pounded off along the Fort Davis road through the darkness. Presently, he swung it to the right, threaded between the dark bulks of sleeping peaks until he found the shadow-blackness of a small canyon. There he took cover, slept for two hours to refresh himself. Then he arose again and was at Hanna's ranch by dawn.

Chapter V

Although Jim Hanna owned more land and ran more cattle than Walt Steed, his headquarters ranch was smaller. Its main house of cottonwood and adobe was built years ago. Inside, it was comfortable, but there was nothing fancy about it.

Hanna in his time had fought rustlers, Indians, and the big die-up of thirty years before, when the roughest Western winter in history had wiped out most of the cattle on the range. In their first conversation, Fargo had caught the difference between him and Steed. Hanna was hard, hard as flint, but he could be trusted; Steed was a different case entirely.

Now, as Fargo ate hungrily of bacon and eggs and drank hot black coffee, Hanna paced the house's dining room. "It started right after you turned us down that day. Until then, Steed and I always ran beeves on that Black Valley range together. Since we were the two biggest cowmen in the district, we tried —I tried, anyhow—to cooperate. No sense in cuttin' each other's throat.

"But then Steed decided to go off on his own.

When you said no thanks, he went to hirin' gunmen. Behind my back, not tellin' me that he was doin' it, and when I finally found out, I knew right away what he was up to. Oh, he figgers on runnin' the Canfields outa Black Valley all right. And then he aims to take it *all* for himself and not give me a sniff of it."

"And what did you decide to do about that?" Fargo swallowed and raised his head.

"What the hell can I do?" Hanna's voice rose; his mustache bristled angrily. "I thought we had given each other our word to let the matter drop, especially after the Canfields killed that Ranger. We agreed that it would be only a matter of time before the Rangers came in and cleaned 'em out, and we could leave it up to them. I was waiting for that, but Walt didn't wait. He went to hiring fighting men and when I asked him what he was up to, he told me it was none of my business."

Hanna stopped pacing, sat down, drank a long jolt of strong coffee. "All the makin's of a first class, oldtime range war, Fargo. The Canfields hold Black Valley, I want it, Steed wants it. If he gets it first, he'll freeze me out. If I could get it first, I'd freeze him out—now. But I ain't got a chance of gettin' it first."

"Why not?"

"Because there's only so many hired gunmen left; we talked about that before. Fighting men are scarce, and what's available, Steed's already got. So he'll go in there and take the Valley and I'm out in the cold, and there's not a thing I can do about it. My riders are good cowpunchers, but they ain't the kind of men it would take to smoke the Canfields out—and maybe go up against Steed's gunnies too."

Taking another swig of coffee, Fargo leaned back and lit a cigarette.

"How much would it be worth to you to have the Canfields cleared out of Black Valley completely and entirely—and for you to get to it first and take it over before Steed does?"

Hanna stared at him. Then his eyes glittered. "A hell of a lot. I've got claims filed on that land, and so has Steed. Possession's nine-tenths of the law. When the title's finally cleared, the man who already holds it is the one with the best chance of winnin'." He leaned forward across the table. "You know where you could find an army to match Steed's?"

"No," Fargo said.

Hanna let out a long breath. "Then what's the use in askin' such a damn fool question?"

Fargo plumed smoke through his nostrils. "Last night, Steed sent men to kill me. The reason he did that was to keep me from comin' to you and makin' any sort of deal with you. Well, I'm ready to make a deal, our original deal. You wanted me to go into Black Valley and clear it out, alone. That's what I'm proposing to do. The trick is, you'll have to bear the whole freight instead of splittin' it with Steed."

"Damn it, Fargo, that's the best piece of range in these whole mountains. I figured for half of it, I could pony up ten thousand dollars. For the whole thing, with Steed out, I could go the entire twenty." Then he snorted. "But you can't do it, now. Before, it was only the Canfields you had to deal with. Now you got to deal with Walt Steed's army, too."

"Then you get two for the price of one," Fargo grinned. "Canfields and Steed."

Hanna stared at him. "You really mean it? You think you, alone, could clear the Canfields out of Black Valley and keep Steed from comin' in until I could take over all that range and hold it myself?"

"I'm making you that offer. For ten thousand

73

dollars now and ten more when your cattle are up there in Black Valley."

"And you're gonna kill all those Canfields and rub out Steed's gunmen?"

"I didn't say who was gonna get killed or how. I said I would clear the Canfields out and see you got possession of the range."

There was a long silence in the room. Hanna looked at Fargo curiously.

"You know," he said at last, "I grew up out here. I have known some wild ones in my time, because I'm pushin' seventy. Wes Hardin, I knew him, and King Fisher, and I've bumped into Earp and the Mastersons. I even seen Hickock once in Abilene, when I was a young-un. Before I went in business for myself, I worked for John Chisum in New Mexico, and I knew the Kid, Billy Bonney, and all the McSween and Dolan gunmen and the Seven Rivers gang. Up in Wyomin', some time ago, I run into Butch Cassidy and Harry Longbaugh and Harvey Logan. I thought I had seen all the tough ones. But here it is, damn near twenty years into the twentieth century, and in all that time I never run up against one like you, Fargo. Not exactly like you."

Fargo said nothing. Only drank coffee.

Hanna got up. "Wait here a minute," he said and left the room.

Fargo finished his coffee, poured more from the pot, swabbed up egg yellow with a piece of bread.

Hanna reappeared. Coming to the table, he said, "Here," and he threw down a thick packet of greenbacks. "Count it. There ought to be ten thousand there."

Fargo riffled the packet of bank-wrapped money. "Exactly," he said, and put it in his coat.

"That's the first payment. When I have exclusive

possession of Black Valley—no Canfields, no Walt Steed—you get the rest."

Fargo smiled. "How many head will that range graze?"

"Seven hundred, easy."

"Make your gather," Fargo said. "Get seven hundred head ready to push up there within four days. Be ready to go on short notice." He ground out his cigarette, doing figures in his head. The range up there would put twenty dollars worth of extra beef on every cow. Fourteen thousand dollars this year, another fourteen the next, and if the price of beef held, fourteen after that. Yeah, he thought. Hanna'll get his money's worth. He stood up. "I'm gonna sleep a spell. I don't think Steed will send any more men after me. But if riders come, wake me up."

"Help yourself," Hanna said. "In there." He pointed to a door.

Fargo hitched the shotgun sling on his shoulder, picked up his Winchester and went into the bedroom. It had been a long time since he had slept in a real bed. He unloaded his hardware, lay down with his boots off on the mattress, and, for seven hours, slept soundlessly without dreams.

Before he left Hanna's ranch, he had memorized the map made by the Army years before. Black Valley and the gorgelike entrance to it, Black Canyon, were firmly fixed in his mind. The Valley itself was really a huge basin rimmed by hills, watered lushly by springfed streams. Through only one notch in the rugged slopes around it could cattle be driven or wagons pass: the canyon.

To approach it, Fargo rode at night. All this range outside the canyon and the valley was scattered with either Steed's Lazy S or Hanna's Oxbow branded cattle. Steed would have hands riding through the mountains and maybe more gunmen. Fargo avoided trouble by traveling exactly as he would have if the mountains still swarmed with Apaches, as they had in times long past.

The second sunrise after leaving Hanna's ranch found him on the slope of a narrow valley that stretched out below and beyond like a corridor, seemingly wholly sealed at its far end by a towering, sheer rock wall hundreds of feet in height. Beyond that wall lay Black Valley. As morning mists cleared, he scanned the cliff with field glasses, shielding their lenses with cupped palms to avoid any glint of reflection that might give away his presence. Presently, he spotted the notch in that apparently blank face of volcanic rock: a narrow gorge cut by some ancient stream long since gone dry. That would be Black Canyon, the only entrance to the domain of the Canfields. He turned the glasses on the gorge's rims. He could not see them, but he knew they were there: mountain men with rifles, guarding the deadline they had laid down for all outsiders.

He turned the sorrel and pushed it back up the valley, circled another peak. He took time to let it graze and rest and water; there was one more hard day's riding ahead of it. During that interval, he ate a can of beans and some jerky, and then he carefully checked his guns again.

In a couple of hours, he hit the saddle once more. He skirted the foot of the peak, keeping to every bit of cover available. He soon was confronted with another barrier. It was an extension of the rock face that made the wall through which the gorge ran, but its slope was not so sheer, here. Its northern end joined with another range of peaks that seemed to run on endlessly.

76

True enough, Fargo thought. The gorge was the only entrance for cattle, wagons, or, for that matter, a man on horseback. But he was not going into the valley on horseback.

He picketed the sorrel, stashed his gear. He took off his cavalry spurs, decided not to burden himself even with a canteen. The Winchester had sling swivels, and he took a sling from his saddlebags and snapped it on. It, the shotgun, his bandoliers, and the Colt made all the weight he cared to carry when he made the climb.

He used the glasses once more, picking out his route in advance, sizing up the cover, willing to zigzag to have the shelter of any overhang that would protect him from fire coming from above. Then, in the lengthening shadows of twilight, he, moved on, crouched low, running toward the escarpment like a hunting wolf, using every low swirl of ground, and every clump of juniper, every stalk of giant yucca that offered shelter, each clump of cactus. Presently, he reached the foot of the wall, dwarfed by its great height. He sucked in a long breath, began the upward climb.

It was not something he enjoyed. Every man had his weak spot, his own private fear: Fargo's was of high places. Twenty, thirty feet off the ground was one thing; a hundred was another. But it was a fear he had long since trained himself to overcome. He could not make it go away, but he could ignore it. He did that now as he started up the wall.

It was bad, but not nearly so bad as trying to make the climb closer to the gorge would have been. He went, as always, with precision and due regard for cover, never letting haste overpower caution. Only once did he misjudge; his booted foot dislodged a loose rock fifty feet up; he slipped, grabbed a handhold. The rock rolled as Fargo pressed against the wall, caught up others in its passage, clattered down the slope in a miniature slide. Fargo waited a long time in the shelter of an outcrop after the sound had died. But nothing happened. He had not really expected anything to happen. With only thirty fighting men, the Canfields could not patrol the whole barrier; their guards would be concentrated at the gorge.

So he began to climb again.

A full hour later, when darkness had settled down, he hoisted himself panting over the rim, lay down flat in the shelter of a clump of juniper to get his breath. He breathed softly, quietly, straining his ears to hear above the thudding of his own heart any voices or other sound of human presence. There was none, so he got to his feet, still hunkered low, holding his weapons and bandoliers with both hands to silence their clicking. Fargo looked around.

The moon had not yet risen, but his night vision was good. He saw that he was on a narrow hogback that ran north and south between two chains of peaks. Eastward, the escarpment fell away below him; not more than a hundred feet to the west, the ridge sloped gently to the immense basin beyond: Black Valley, the Canfield country. The gorge and the guards were to the south, fully two miles away.

It took him another two hours to cover those two miles. By then, the moon was up, flooding the narrow ridge with silver, lighting up the breathtaking vastness of the basin beyond, painting with shadows and brightness all this enormous, jumbled country.

Fargo was traveling on his belly now, not more than a couple of hundred feet from where the gorge sliced through the wall. He made fifty feet more like that, silently as a rattlesnake, and came to rest behind a stunted, wind-warped juniper. From that cover, he scanned the gorge's rim, turning his head slowly from side to side, Indian fashion, the pupils of his eyes remaining stationary.

Then he saw the Canfield.

Behind the shelter of a pile of rocks at the gorge's very rim, where its floor and the outer valley both could be kept under observation, the man lay sprawled on a blanket. He wore no jacket despite the chill of the wind up here, and the straps of bib overalls crisscrossed his back over a homespun shirt. Once, when he shifted position slightly, Fargo caught the silhouette of an uptilted rifle barrel, recognized a Sharps .50 caliber buffalo gun. Beside the guard, on the blanket, was a box of heavy cartridges. Also close at hand, removed for comfort, was a cartridge belt and a holstered Colt.

Fargo waited. Vigils like this were lonely. If there was another guard anywhere around, he would sooner or later call out to him.

Time passed: fifteen minutes, thirty. The Canfield sat up, tilted back his slouch hat. Then he gave a soft, low whistle.

Fargo held his breath.

An answering whistle came from the opposite gorge wall. Then the Canfield in front of Fargo called out, still softly: "Buck. Ever'thang quiet over thar?"

"Like a grave, Rafe."

"Thought mebbe you'd gone to sleep."

"You know better'n thet. Daddy come up hyar, find us asleep, he'd mortally tear the hide offn us."

"Yeah," Rafe chuckled. Fargo guessed that these were two of Roaring Tom's sons, Jess's older brothers. "Yeah, he'd feather into us good. Well, I'm gonna smoke a pipe." He laid down his rifle. Fargo watched him pull out pipe and tobacco pouch, and Fargo's mouth made its wolf's snarl. His hand went to his hip, fished the Batangas knife from its sheath.

Soundlessly, the folded handles whipped back to expose the ten-inch blade as he jerked his wrist. Then, while the Canfield was intent on tamping his pipe, he jumped to his feet and made the run.

Crouched low, elbows holding his bandoliers to still their clicking, knife outthrust in his left hand, he was a silent blur. The Canfield thrust his pipe in his mouth, wholly unaware. Then Fargo was on him. His right arm shot out, clamped around the Canfield's throat, choking off all outcry. He stuck the knifepoint into the Canfield's back—not far, just deep enough to let him feel the prick. His voice was a whisper in Rafe's ear. "You move, you squawk, you're dead."

For a moment, he thought he'd have to use the blade. Then Rafe relaxed in his grip.

"Back," Fargo whispered. "Away from the edge. You reach for a gun, it'll be your last reach. And keep down low."

They hitched away from the gorge's rim. Rafe, intimidated by that knife point, had better sense than to try to struggle. Fargo's arm was like an iron band around his neck. They were soon in the shadow of a clump of juniper.

"Now, you behave yourself," Fargo rasped, "you're all right. My name's Neal Fargo. I fought your brother in Fort Davis, you remember? Your daddy promised me safe conduct into Black Valley any time I wanted it because I didn't stomp him to death. I ain't going to kill you, either, unless you make me. What I want you to do is take me to Roaring Tom. And make damned sure no trigger-happy Canfield picks me off on the way. You understand?"

Rafe managed enough head motion to signify a nod. Fargo loosened the clamp a little. "Where's your horse?"

"Mule . . . down yonder." Rafe swallowed, trying to get his voice working again. "Ye don't need—put up that knife. Daddy'd skin me . . . alive, iffn . . . any harm come to ye, after . . . he done give his word."

Fargo hesitated; then he swung his wrist. The handles folded forward across the blade and he latched them, returned the Batangas knife to its sheath. But his other hand pulled his Colt, held it ready, as he released Rafe's throat.

Rafe hitched around to look him in the face, still rubbing his neck. He was an older, though not harder, version of Jess Canfield. "By God, hit is you. I recollect that soldier hat." Slowly he raised his hands. "Awright, Mister. You don't need to hold that there pistol on me. I tell you, Canfields keep their word. I'll take you to Daddy and make sure you git to him plumb safe."

Fargo stared at him for a moment, appraising the short-bearded face in the moonlight. Then he rammed the pistol back in leather. "Okay," he said. "Move on down the slope, to the mule. But I warn you now, any tricks and—"

"There won't be no tricks, I done told ye. Ye think I'm fool enough to go up unarmed against a man whut could whup Jess and sneak up on me and take me like I was some little baby? I tell ye, Mister Fargo, ye're safe here in Black Valley. Daddy's sworn word's good for ever' Canfield here. Only thing I wonder is why ye snuck up behind me instid o' comin' through the canyon straight up."

"Because I didn't want to be blown out of the saddle before you recognized me. The way I hear it, you Canfields are shootin' first and askin' questions later."

Rafe's face clouded. "Maybe ever'thang ye hear ain't true." Then he got to his feet. "Come on," he said, still rubbing his throat. "I'll take ye down to the settlement."

They rode double on a tall, strong mule that carried both of them without difficulty. It took them down the slope, deep into the basin. In the moonlight, Fargo could see that, indeed, at least a hundred acres of the rangeland on the valley floor had been plowed, and scraggly corn was growing on it. When they reached the level, they struck a cart trail and turned right in the shadow of the ridge. Presently, ahead, Fargo saw a scattering of buildings. As they drew near he made out that they were cabins, built of hewn post-oak, cedar and cottonwood logs. Four or five of them, with barns and pens, were clustered around one much larger than the rest. At their approach, there was the sudden blare of barking dogs, the baying of great hounds. A pack of huge animals, black and tan, came roaring out from behind the bigger building, swarmed around the mule.

"Hush, Track, Trigger, Trail, Trap . . ." Rafe's voice quieted them. "Daddy's bear dawgs," he said. "We brung 'em from the East when we come out hyar. Ye better wait 'til I git shed of them. Ye git down off this mule, they'll eat ye alive afore ye can blink." He swung down, cuffing and shoving at the dogs. Meanwhile, light flared in the bigger cabin; a wooden shutter slapped open and the long barrel of a Kentucky rifle rammed through. "What the devil's goin' on out thar?"

"Hit's Rafe, Pappy. I got somebody with me—thet feller Fargo, thet whupped Jess in Fort Davis! Says he wants to see ye!"

The other houses were lit, now. Men swarmed out carrying guns. The door of Roaring Tom's cabin opened. He was there in nightshirt and boots, his

82

rifle trained on Fargo, his long beard fluttering in the breeze. Behind him came Jess and three others, and they all carried guns.

"Fargo, is it?" the old man bellowed. He stalked up to him, peered into his face. "Yeah. Hit's ye. What brings ye here?"

"The way I heard it, I was welcome any time."

"So ye be. Jest the same—" Then Jess had shoved up past him, confronted Fargo. The younger Canfield held a revolver in each hand.

"So ye come back to try again, huh? Well, this time, hit won't be fists and ye won't ketch me with my boot half off." Jess's eyes glittered in the moonlight. "I got a score to settle with ye, feller, and ye better—"

"Hush." Roaring Tom stepped between the muzzles of Jess's guns and Fargo. "I bid this man welcome, and hit's welcome he is. Put up them pistols, son."

Jess's lips peeled back from his teeth. "No! He whupped me once when I couldn't fight on accounta thet boot! He totes a lotta hardware, let's see how he kin use hit." His voice rose. "All of y'all stand back. Pappy, git outa my path."

"I said, put up them guns. This man's a guest hyar."

"And I said, move!" Jess took a step forward.

Then Roaring Tom hit him. His hand was huge; it flashed back, then forward, palm open. The slap would have stunned a bear. It sent Jess reeling, and, despite his age, the old man was panther quick. He caught Jess's wrists, squeezed; Fargo thought he heard the grate of bone on bone. The two guns dropped as Jess snarled in pain.

Roaring Tom stooped, scooped them up, passed them quickly to Rafe. Jess stood there staring at him, rubbing his face, already beginning to swell from that tremendous, open-handed blow. "Pappy," he said in a voice of fury, "don't ye ever hit me like thet again. I'm a man full-growed. Don't ye ever—"

"Hush yer trap!" said Roaring Tom in a voice like ice, "and git inside."

"I—" Jess broke off. His eyes locked with those of his father for a full ten seconds. His big fists were clenched. Then he let out a long breath. Wordlessly, he turned, strode into the cabin.

Roaring Tom watched him go. It was as if, having forgotten Fargo, he suddenly remembered. He turned. "I apologize. When I say a man's welcome hyar, he's welcome, until he abuses our hospitality. Come inside, Bonnie will fix ye a bait of vittles."

The cabin's front room was big, its floor of hard-packed dirt, its fireplace, in which embers smoldered, of mountain stone. A huge spinning wheel sat on one side of it, an old-fashioned handloom on the other. A cougar's tawny hide made a rug before the hearth, and there were guns everywhere. The place was a veritable arsenal: rifles, revolvers, shotguns, hung on pegs or were stacked in corners. Nor did Fargo miss the cans of powder, the boxes of cartridges for the modern weapons. Apparently this was not only the clan's headquarters, but its fort. Heavy wooden shutters, thick enough to stop a bullet, guarded every window; loopholes and firing slits pierced the walls.

Tom gestured to a board table with split-log benches. "Set," he said. Tallow candles burned in holders, and in their flickering light, his eyes raked over Fargo and his armament. "Jess was right. Ye do tote a lot of hardware."

"I use it in my business."

"Which is?"

"Fighting," Fargo said.

84

Tom nodded. "I figgered that back in Fort Davis. I got a feelin' Jess is lucky I stopped him from going up against ye. Bonnie! Bonnie!"

The girl appeared in a doorway at the end of the room. She was clad in a tattered flannel robe belted around her waist with a piece of rope. Her hair hung down in a thick, loosened, glittering cascade around her shoulders. Her blue eyes widened at the sight of Fargo.

"Fix this gentleman something to eat."

"Yes, Pappy," she said. Fargo carefully kept his eyes off of her as she went to the fireplace. Next to Jess, she spelled worse trouble than any other Canfield in the valley.

Roaring Tom dismissed the other men who hovered around curiously. "Awright, dadburn it! Don't stand thar like blackbirds on a fence. Ye, Joe-Sam, git back up yonder and take Rafe's place! Willie, ye go relieve Buck! The rest of ye git back to bed; we got work to do early in the mornin'! And ye two guards—keep yer eyes open! Don't let nobody else take ye like no sucklin' babe!"

They mumbled assent, drifted out. Tom went to a shelf, brought back a two-gallon clay demijohn, uncorked it, shoved it at Fargo. "Have a snort. Then we got talkin' to do."

Fargo hooked a thumb through the handle, cradled the jug on his bent arm, hoisted it and drank without spilling a drop. Tom grinned. " 'Pears like ye're as good with a jug as with yer fists."

He took the demijohn, drank, too. Then he snorted, wiped his beard. "Okay, Mr. Fargo. Whut brings ye to Black Valley?"

"I got some bad news for you," Fargo said.

"Oh? Whut is hit?" Tom's face didn't change. In the candlelight, it was like a relief map of a rugged mountain range itself, all peaks and wrinkled valleys.

"You know a man named Steed?"

"I know him," Tom growled. "Land-grabbing bastard. Wusser than a Whipple."

"He's getting up an army. He's coming in here to clean you out."

Tom sat immobile for a moment. Then he picked up the squirrel rifle, laid it on the table before him. "Oh, is he now?" His big hands caressed the long barrel, the polished, silver-mounted stock. "Well, I allow we can take keer of him."

"Maybe not," Fargo said. "He'll have fifty men. Top guns. I know the man who's leading them. He's been around a long time and knows his business."

Roaring Tom spat on the dirt floor, rubbed it with his boot. "They cain't get through thet pass."

"*I* didn't come through that pass." He reached for the jug. "If I can take your guard out, what makes you think Steed's men can't do the same?"

"Hit won't happen twice. If hit does, I'll have some hides around hyar."

"You've got thirty men; Steed's got fifty, maybe more. And there's law coming on top of them—the Texas Rangers. If Steed's men don't get you, the Rangers will." He drank, set down the jug, looked at Roaring Tom directly and with unwavering eyes. "Because Jess killed a Ranger."

Tom's eyes shifted. "He didn't know hit was a badge-toter."

"He didn't know that man of Steed's he killed was just a cowboy, either, huh? It don't make much difference to Jess who he kills, does it?"

Tom was silent for a moment. "Hit's his mother's blood," he said at last, almost wearily. "She was my second wife. Ye seed her in Fort Davis."

"Yes." Fargo remembered the old crone.

"She was always . . . a little peculiar. She . . . died last month."

"I'm sorry," Fargo said.

Tom shrugged. "My first wife birthed the other boys. She borned Bonnie and Jess. Bonnie is wild and so's he. But he's a different kind of wild. Mean wild." He grabbed the jug, drank long and deeply. "All us Canfields is wild, but Jess is the onliest one thet's mean." Dragging his hand across his beard, he went on. "Thet's not yer affair, though. Let 'em come. Let 'em all come. We'll stand 'em off." But that weariness lingered in his voice, mingled with a kind of sadness. "I tole Jess never to shoot without he challenged a man first and made him state his business, but . . . well, no matter. We're in hit, now; we'll fight our way out. Or go down trying."

"You'll go down," Fargo said. "You might beat Steed's men, but you can't lick the Rangers."

"Goddamn it," Canfield burst out, "whut else is thar? We run out of the Smoky Mountains on account of the Whipples went to the law and sent it agin us. We come to these damned hills thet ain't nothin' like the ones we're used to, but we're tryin' to make do in 'em, if folks would only let us alone. I'm tired of fightin'. I been fightin' Whipples all my life, like my pappy and his pappy before me fit 'em. All the same, thur's fight left in me. Plenty of it. Besides, if we git run outa hyar, we got nowhur else to go."

"Maybe," Fargo said. "Maybe not."

He got up, thrusting a cigarette into his mouth. Bonnie looked up at him as he bent, seized an ember, lit it. He disregarded her, turned to face Roaring Tom.

"I've been in the Smokies where you come from," he said quietly. "I know what they're like. The big woods and the water runnin' outa living rock, the fog on the mountains in the morning, the land all straight up and down, lonesome and wild. Trees everywhere, dark woods, spruce and poplar and hickory and oak . . ."

"Shet up," Tom said. "Ye're makin' me homesick. I love thet land. It tore my guts to leave it."

"The Davis Mountains aren't much like the Smokies," Fargo said. "Scrub juniper and cactus ain't much like big timber. It's good grazing land for cattle, but not much for farming."

"Don't I know it. But, like I said, thar's no whur else to go."

Fargo blew a plume of smoke. "You ever been down in the Sierra Madre?"

"Whar's thet?"

"Mexico. Sonora, Chihuahua, Durango. Mountains that run on for a thousand miles. There's places in there never been explored, canyons you could put this whole range of hills in. Peaks high enough so there's snow year round, valleys low and fertile. Big timber and game, lots of game. Deer, cougar, bear, wild turkey, quail, wild hogs."

"Man," Roaring Tom said. "Man alive."

"A whole world of mountains. And nobody in 'em except a few Mexicans and some harmless Indians. There's silver in there, and gold. Water, plenty of it . . ."

He came to the table, bent low, face close to Roaring Tom's. "I know a valley down there just made for a family like yours. It don't show up on any maps. I think I'm the only white man that's ever seen it." His eyes gleamed, his voice was earnest, intense. "There's big timber, pine and oak and pinon, all up the slopes. Good, rich bottomland that would grow fine corn, and a fast, cold stream runnin' through it. There's range, too, for sheep and cattle, and you could fatten hogs up in the pinons and the

88

oaks. And the wild turkeys are thick as fleas. There's signs of silver on one wall, and a coal outcrop on the other. Everything a clan like yours could want. Coffee, sugar, flour and bullets, that kind of stuff—one trip outside every six months, no more . . ."

He straightened up. "The mountains around it are high and lonesome, like the Smokies. Hot in daytime, chilly at night. There's a waterfall two hundred feet high at one end, and a big pool where it hits, and a grove there to shelter houses. You could climb up on the peaks and look down on the clouds. The fog hangs low there until ten o'clock, and you can hear sounds from twenty miles away. It's a fine place, Tom Canfield—and I could lead you there, you and your family."

The old man stared at him. "Lord God Almighty," he whispered. "It sounds like the promised land. Who are ye? Moses?"

"Only Fargo." He hoisted the jug, drank, smacked his lips. "And the Mexicans, the Revolutionists, know Neal Fargo. I've sold them guns and ammo, hauled out their silver to market, trained their troops. And they're gonna win, Canfield. Villa, Carranzo, Obregon and the rest. They're gonna lick the government and take that country over. And they owe me favors, lots of favors. I could collect. By making sure that the Canfields could settle in the Sierra under their protection."

The old man just kept on staring at Fargo. Then Bonnie put down a plate and cup beside him on the table. "Here's ye vittles, Mr. Fargo." She bent, turned away from her father as she served him. Roaring Tom could not see how the neck of the gown fell away, revealing her breasts in total, lovely nakedness. But Fargo could.

He glanced, then coldly turned his face away. She straightened up, cheeks reddening.

"Man," Roaring Tom whispered. "Man alive, this place, Fargo, this valley. Ye ain't lying?"

"I don't lie," Fargo said. "It's exactly like I described."

Canfield licked his lips. "And what would be yer price for leadin' us thar before Steed or the Rangers could hit us? Showin' us thet place and arrangin' with the Mexicans for us to settle hit."

"My price?" Fargo said. He glanced at Bonnie, then jerked his thumb. "Send her out of the room so we can talk private."

"Get to bed, child," Roaring Tom rasped, not even looking at her.

"Pappy—"

"I said git to bed or I'll strap ye good!"

She hesitated, shot Fargo a resentful glance, then flounced out, buttocks shifting exaggeratedly, deliberately, beneath the robe. She slammed the door behind her.

Now they were alone in the big room. "Well?" Tom stared at Fargo. "The price? What is it?"

Fargo took the cigarette from his mouth.

"I want Jess," he said.

Chapter VI

Except for the popping of the fire in the hearth, the big room was silent.

"Jess," Roaring Tom said at last, his craggy face seemingly frozen, his eyes gone icy. "Whut do ye mean, ye want Jess?"

"I want to take him into Fort Davis for trial for killing that Texas Ranger."

Tom looked at him blankly for a moment. Then he stood up slowly. "So thet's it," he grated, and he swung the Kentucky rifle and eared back the hammer. Its muzzle pointed at Fargo's belly. "So all this time, a guest in my house, ye was nothin' but a stinkin' lawman, come under cover of my friendship! Abusin' the hospitality and trust! The law—"

"No," Fargo said, not moving. "I'm not the law. But I'm doing a job for the law."

"It makes no difference. No never-mind at all. Ye want to take my baby boy down thar whur they can hang him." Canfield's voice trembled with growing fury.

"Canfield," Fargo said, still immobile, displaying no fear. "Listen to me."

"I don't listen to sneakin'—"

"You listen." Fargo's voice was flat, commanding. "Your son Jess killed a Texas Ranger. He would have done better to climb the tallest tree on the highest peak out yonder wearing a copper hat and copper boots in the middle of a thunderstorm, because he's drawn down the lightnin' on himself—and on you. The Rangers will never rest until they've had him. And if they have to kill you all to get him, they will."

"Then let them come," Tom grated. "Lotta good it'll do ye, ye stool pigeon—"

"I'm no stool pigeon. I'm the only man who could have walked in here and talked to you like this, made you this deal that will save you and your family from being wiped out—and will save a lot of Rangers, too. The Rangers are tied up now, they can't come now, but they will, sooner or later. And if you don't deal with me, you ain't got a prayer. Not you nor any of your other sons, nor your brothers nor your nephews. You came here to escape the Whipples. But what the Rangers will do to you will make the Whipples look like old ladies at a tea party."

"No Canfield's goin' before no court of law! Whut we came hyar for was to get away from law—"

"Well, you can't do it. There's nowhere you can, except down in the Sierra Madre—"

He sucked in a deep breath. Canfield's face was still twisted with rage; his finger was on the trigger.

"Let me take Jess in. He'll have a fair trial."

"And they'll hang him."

"If he shot a Ranger in the back, yeah."

Roaring Tom shook his head savagely. "No! Even if he did, I'll not see him hanged like some damned chicken-killin' dog! Not a Canfield man!" His voice rose. "What do ye think I am, Fargo? Ye think I'd trade off my own son for a piece of land, some lousy valley in the Mexican mountings?"

"It's the only way, Tom Canfield. Give me Jess, that takes care of the Rangers. Once he's in Fort Davis, I'll move you out before Steed's men come and you won't have to fight 'em. Or if they hit before you leave, I'll fight alongside you against them, if it comes to that. I know Lin Gordon, the man who leads them. I know how he operates. I can outguess him in a way you can't."

"Ye got the brass of a Goddamned monkey," Canfield whispered.

"No," Fargo said. "If I had any sense, I would have Injuned in here and holed up in the brush and waited for my chance. I would have picked off Jess from ambush and as many other Canfields as it took to get clear again, and you'd never have even known who the killer was. And whatever was left of your family then could have faced Steed's men without any advance warnin' at all." He paused. "Don't pull that trigger. I want another cigarette."

"Take hit," Canfield rasped.

Fargo did, and lit it from the candle.

"That's what I would have done if I'd had sense. But the trouble is, Tom, in a way, I'm a Canfield, too. The less law around me, the better I like it; and I'm more comfortable in the lonesome places in this world than I am in the biggest cities. I'm just enough Canfield myself so that I don't feel that people like you ought to be stamped out just because one of you has turned rogue and started backshootin' ...."

"Backshootin's the way it's done back home."

'Not out here. It makes no difference, now. I reckon I was a fool for wantin' to save this wild-assed family of yours from being rubbed out to the last man. All right," he said. "I'll make you another proposition."

"Whut?"

"Jess wants to fight me again. Let him try it. Any way, with any weapon. Pistols, knives, rifles, it makes no difference. Let him fight me, square on and man to man. And let it be like the last time in Fort Davis: win or lose, there it ends."

"No," Tom said. His eyes ran over Fargo's guns. "No. He's tough. But not like ye. Ye've been around, ye're older, smarter. Ye'd kill him."

"I could have killed him in Fort Davis. If I kill him now . . . at least he'll have had an even break. And that will satisfy the Rangers. And then I'll take the rest of you to the Sierra Madre." He smiled wryly. "If I'm still alive."

There was a long moment, then, when Roaring Tom stared hard at him. The candle flames on the table wavered, flickered and reflected in the old man's eyes; and in that interval Fargo knew he was as close to death as he had ever been. Not even *he* could unlimber one of the weapons that hung on him before the ball from that long old flintlock plowed through his belly, if Tom Canfield squeezed the trigger one ounce harder.

Their eyes locked, his and those of the old patriarch of this wild clan. Then, after what seemed years, Canfield let out a long breath that fluttered mustache and beard.

"I ain't goin' to kill ye now," he said. "The reason I ain't is because ye let Jess live when ye had him at yer mercy in Fort Davis. But I'm goin' to tell ye to take off all them guns. Slow and easy. And no tricks. This gun's been used a long time, and it's trigger-action's slick and easy. The fustest trick, and ye're a dead man fer shore." His voice crackled. "Take off them guns."

"All right," Fargo said. He did so, very carefully. He unslung the shotgun, laid it on the table. Then the rifle. He unstrapped the cartridge belt, put the .38 beside the long guns. Fishing out the Batangas knife, he laid it beside them. "That does it," he said. "I'm slick."

Holding the rifle level with one hand, Tom scooped up each weapon in turn, backed across the room, laid it in a corner. "Now," he said, when the table was clear of guns. "Set down and eat."

"Sure," Fargo said. He lowered himself to the bench, attacked the food with gusto.

Roaring Tom kept the rifle pointing at him, but when the old man spoke, it was almost as if to himself.

"A hunderd years," he said. "Thet's how long the feud went on, how long we fit the Whipples. Whut started it? Nobody remembers now. The story is a Whipple dawg killed my great-gran'pappy's chickens. My grandsire killed the dawg. The Whipple it belonged to bushwhacked him for thet. And my own daddy killed the Whipple thet done it.

"And so it went on," he said wearily. "A life fer a life, a man fer a man, like an endless circle, a snake swallowin' itself, nowhar to break hit, end hit. Until hit warn't safe to ride a road through them mountains. The Whipples got my two youngest brothers and I shot two of them myself from a laurel hell whar I was holed up, knocked 'em over while they was cuttin' wood, their guns laid aside. And then they killed my older brother and . . . and on and on . . .

"Until times changed. Until they saw they was losin' and went to the law. And when the law come in a-lookin' fer us, I knowed thet finally it was broken. Thet we couldn't fight the law, not the whole state. And so we pulled out. We come to Texas be-

97

cause we heerd the law was slim out hyar. We found this land two years ago and settled on hit. Wantin' only to be left alone . . ."

He spat. "Then Steed. Steed and Hanna. They wouldn't leave us be. Had to crowd us, push us. And so Jess shot Steed's rider. And thet brought in the Ranger and Jess shot him. And now thet brings in ye and probably I'll have to kill ye and then . . . All over again. Goddamn it, all over again, jest like it was before."

Fargo drank hot coffee.

"I got to think," Tom said. "I got to think whut to do. Meanwhile, when ye finish eatin', I'm gonna lock ye up. Ye won't be harmed, not yit. But I got to decide whut I'm gonna do with ye. I got to think on this and pray on hit and talk to my brothers on hit, and then I got to do whutever hit looks like I have to. Meanwhile, ye'd better not try to run and ye'd better not touch a far-arn. Ye do, and we'll shoot ye down and thet'll be the end of ye."

"All right," Fargo said. "You think about it. But don't think too long. Steed will be coming soon, and the Rangers won't be far behind."

When he had finished eating, Roaring Tom motioned him to his feet, led him outside around the cabin to a log lean-to that was an offshoot of the structure. "Sometimes a feller'll git drunk and ructious and we hafta lock him up. This hyar's our jail. Thar's blankets and a mattress in thar, and it won't do ye no good to try to git out. Them logs is sot deep in the ground and they're a foot through. Ye'd need a choppin' ax and two days time to make a hole. In ye go." He unlocked the door, prodded Fargo through with the muzzle of the gun. "I'll be back to talk to ye in the mornin'."

Fargo just had time to locate the bed and blankets. Then the heavy door of notched logs slammed

98

shut behind him; a padlock clicked. He was in total darkness. He groped his way to the cot, lay down. Suddenly he was profoundly tired. There was no time to kick off his boots before sleep claimed him.

He slept through the night.

What awakened him the next morning was the sound of gunfire.

Fargo sat up quickly in the darkness of the little room, reaching instinctively for weapons that weren't there. Then he relaxed; the rhythmic tempo of the firing told him that the Canfields were taking target practice, just as the gunmen at Steed's ranch had done. The practice was important; no matter how naturally talented a marksman might be, without that frequent exercise of eye and reflex, that sharpening of his gunspeed, he grew rusty. And a rusty gunman was soon dead.

It went on and on, and his ears identified the sound of the different weapons; the slap of Winchester, the deep cough of sixgun, and the deeper roar, even, of the muzzle-loaders and the Sharps buffalo guns. Fargo tucked in his shirttail, clamped the cavalry hat on his close-cropped white hair. Then he heard someone fumbling at the lock, and the door opened.

Roaring Tom was there, squirrel rifle under his arm, its muzzle loosely trained on Fargo. "Mornin'," he said coolly. "I reckon ye'd like to git out and move around and have some breakfast."

Fargo nodded.

"I want yer word ye won't try no tricks, pick no fight with Jess, reach fer no gun. Ye give me that, ye kin come out. Otherwise, this is whar ye stay until we decide whut we-uns are gonna do with ye."

"You've got my word," Fargo said.

"I didn't mention whut ye told me last night to

nobody yet. Ye ain't to mention hit, neither. Ye understand?"

Fargo nodded.

"Then come on out." Roaring Tom stepped back.

Outdoors, Fargo blinked in the wine-colored light of early mountain morning. On the other side of the settlement, the shooting continued. He could see the Canfield men, down to boys no older than twelve, standing at a kind of firing line. Beyond them, far away, a succession of cedar posts had been set up on the valley floor—two hundred, three, four, five hundred yards. The white squares of targets were tiny on the farthest ones. A Canfield on a mule rode back and forth, replacing used targets with fresh ones as necessary. After each round, he blew a blast or two on a steer-horn trumpet like Tom's, evidently in some code that told the marksman where his slug had hit.

"Let's step over thar a minute," Roaring Tom said. He gestured Fargo toward the firing line.

The shooting dwindled as the Canfields became aware of his presence. Bearded, some barefoot, they turned, looking him over curiously; and their eyes were hard. Their whole aspect was as savage as any jungle tribes Fargo had run into in South and Central America or the Philippines. Jess stepped forward from among them, his Henry rifle in his hands. His eyes glittered as they raked over Fargo.

"I see ye took his guns away," he said, derisively.

"He gave up his guns," Roaring, Tom snapped. "He's hyar on private business with me. He's give his promise not to w'ar no hardware whilst he's in the Valley. In turn, I give mine he won't be harmed. Ye understand, Jess?"

Jess Canfield's mouth twisted contemptuously. "A man that'd give up his guns ain't worth botherin' with. Likely he couldn't shoot 'em anyhow. I figgered all along they was jest fer looks." He spat into the dust at Fargo's boots.

"Jess—" Tom began in a voice of warning. Jess's eyes shuttled to his father. They contained only a little less hatred than Fargo had been the object of, and it was obvious that there was a deeper conflict than he had guessed between the old man and his son. Whatever Roaring Tom felt for Jess, the boy did not reciprocate. Probably he could feel nothing for anyone but himself.

Fargo hadn't meant to speak. But Jess's mocking face and bearing rubbed him' raw. "I'd like to try a shot with Jess," he said harshly. "Against a target."

"No! I said ye wasn't to have a hand on no gun!"

Fargo pointed at the old Kentucky rifle. "That single-shot. I ain't likely to try any fancy tricks with one bullet and twenty of you coverin' me. Or is that Henry all Jess knows how to shoot?"

"By God, I teethed on a squirrel gun!" Jess flared. He seized the rifle from Tom's hands before the old man knew what he was about, passed his Henry to a young boy nearby. "Come up here, Fargo."

Fargo glanced at Tom. The old man's face was clouded, black with anger. But he nodded. "All right," he said. "One shot each."

Covered by all those guns, Fargo moved up to the firing line. Jess pointed. "Ye see thet third post yonder? Three hundred yards. Thet target on it's a playin' card cut in half. If I hit it dead center, Leroy down yonder'll blow one long toot on thet horn of his." He threw the long rifle to his shoulder; its stock had hardly seated itself before he pulled the trigger. The roar of the gun was thunderous, and white powder smoke made a fog around its muzzle. Before it swirled away, there came from downrange a single drawn-out mournful blast from the steer's horn.

"Jess turned, grinning triumphantly. He thrust the empty gun at Fargo. "All right, Mister Big Ugly. Let's see whut ye kin do. Give him yer powder horn, Pappy, one ball, and a patch."

Fargo took the long rifle, hefted it. The balance was superb; it was a fine example of the art of the Pennsylvania gunsmiths who had made the best of such weapons. It seemed to float in his hand. He smiled faintly. As a kid of ten or twelve on the ranch of his foster parents, such a gun had been the only one he'd been allowed to use. The penny-pinching man who'd taken him in refused to let him use a cartridge rifle; cartridges cost too much money. Fargo had molded his own bullets, mixed his own powder, even as a child, and had become expert with an ancient musket far less accurate and balanced than the weapon he now held.

Everybody watched in silence now as he raised the empty gun, lined it, got its feel. Then he turned to Roaring Tom. "How's she hold?"

"Dead on," said Tom, "at a hundred yards." His curiosity was getting the better of his caution. He pulled a round ball of about .38 caliber and a patch from his pouch. Along with the powder horn, he passed them over. "One shot," he said firmly. "And no tricks."

"One shot and no tricks." Fargo stripped the ramrod from beneath the barrel. He unplugged the powder horn. "Storebought standard powder or homemade?"

"Homemade," Tom said. "We make ever'thang at home we kin. Thet's to my own receipt." There was growing respect in his eyes. The quality of the powder, the proper charging of the gun according to its strength, was as important in shooting the weapon as the accuracy of the sighting.

Fargo nodded, poured out a touch of powder on his palm. He bent his head, licked the black grains with his tongue. It was a trick he had learned long ago when he made his own powder; the final test was tasting; he knew what a good mixture of sulphur, saltpeter and charcoal should taste like.

Now long-forgotten knowledge returned; his senses assessed Tom's mixture and told him the proportion of ingredients the old man had used, and this in turn gave him some idea of the powder's strength. He uncapped the charger from the horn, measured carefully. A little too much was better than not enough. He added another dab, saw the glint of admiration in the old man's eyes that told him he had used precisely the right charge. His taste, and assessment of the size of the grain, had been exactly right. He wrapped the ball in its greased patch and rammed it in, all done with speed and deftness. Then he charged the priming pan with more black powder, eared back the flint-tipped hammer, raised the gun. Meanwhile, he had been assessing the direction and strength of wind.

The marvelous old weapon seemed to possess a life of its own. Like an animal recognizing its master, it seemed to want to snuggle to his shoulder, float in his hands. He drew a fine bead, holding high to compensate for bullet drop over the extra two hundred yards; and his finger caressed the silken-actioned trigger as the sights came into line.

The long gun roared and kicked and made its fog of smoke. Drifting before Fargo's eyes, it obscured the target and what went on downrange. But as it swirled away, the man on the mule had stripped off the target, was pounding up the range, the square of paper in his hand. He reined the animal to a skittering halt, handed Roaring Tom the target. The old man squinted at it, then grinned. "Awright, Jess; that's yer answer."

Young Canfield's face darkened as he stared at the target. Two holes overlapped in it, making a kind of figure eight. Leroy, the target tender, indicated the lower one. "Thet thar's the fust one fired. Jess's, I reckon. Hit was jest a shade low, but hit still looked like a bullseye. Until the second one hit." There was respect in his eyes as he glanced at Fargo. "They ain't no question 'bout thet un. Hit is purely in the exact middle. Jess ye done been outshot." From the way he grinned, and from the murmur that went through the crowd, Fargo guessed at once that nobody was sorry that Jess had been bested. Apparently the other Canfields bore no great love for him.

Roaring Tom took back his gun, deftly recharged it. "Awright, Mr. Fargo. Ye whupped him fa'r and squar' with the rifle, too. Jess, maybe thet'll teach ye not to run yer mouth so much." He turned away. "Come on, Fargo. Ye're due some coffee and some vittles." As they walked toward the big cabin, Fargo could feel the pressure of the silent Jess's eyes upon his back and the short hair at his neck's nape prickled. He was glad the other Canfields were watching Jess; he was not a man to turn your back on when he held a gun.

"After ye eat," old Tom said, "we'll ride out to the still. I got to check hit—and hit'll give us a chance to talk some more."

The still was near the stream that poured through Black Valley. Six big wooden vats of fermenting corn filled the air with a yeasty tang. Men tended a fire under a huge copper boiler, from which steam wound through long, twisted copper tubing—the worm. It then went through cooling barrels to a condenser from which clear, white corn whiskey trickled. Roaring Tom and Fargo reined in their mules, and Tom shifted the muzzle loader slightly; all the way out here it had been in position to knock Fargo out of the saddle if he had made the least false move. "Light," Tom said and swung down. Fargo followed suit.

Tom inspected the still. "More water in thet mash, thar and keep thet vat covered. Don't want the stuff fulla bugs or no critters crawlin' in and drownin'. And keep thet far a leetle hotter under the b'iler. This is third run; we want hit full stren'th like the other." He turned to Fargo. "Third run's smoothest, best. First two runs, they cook out the impurities in the mash; third run's sweet." He picked up a fruit jar, then gestured with the rifle. "Let's go set."

Out of earshot of the half dozen Canfields at the still, he dropped to a log, unholstering his big Navy Colt and putting it beside him with a significant glance of warning at Fargo. He uncapped the jar, passed it over. Fargo drank, savoring the smooth, potent corn, passed it back. Old Tom drank deeply, watching Fargo over the jar's rim.

He sighed, set down the jar. "I laid awake all night long," he said, "thinkin' about whut ye told me. Thet was the straight goods, about thet valley down in Mexico?"

"Straight," said Fargo.

"I figgered. Ye didn't have the look of a man who'd lie. Not about a thing like thet. And . . . Steed's army, these gunslingers of his. They're comin' atter us? Fer sure?"

"Yeah," Fargo said. "And even if you whip them, then you got the Rangers." He stood up.

"Maybe you ain't been out here long enough to

learn about the Rangers. I tried to tell you about 'em last night. Once a man becomes a Ranger, he's a member of a clan just as tightly bound together as this one, yours. That is why one Ranger can do what it would take an army to, why he can walk into some hell town and cool it off maybe without firin' a shot. Because everybody knows that if they kill a Ranger, hell itself ain't big enough to hide in. Even if you beat Steed's men—and I don't think you can —when the Rangers get loose from the border, they will come up here after Jess. And you will have to kill 'em to stop them from taking him. And after that, they'll send more, and the more you kill, the more will keep coming. They won't stop until they have hanged or killed every one of you for every one of theirs. But they aren't looking for a war like that, and that's why I'm here. To keep one from happening. But you got to figure this, Tom. One way or the other, Jess is a dead man. He may be walking around with that Henry under his arm, but he is dead. And nothing you can do will save him. Absolutely nothing."

Tom sucked in his breath. "That's the hell of hit," he said. "Thet's whut I laid awake all night thinkin' about, Fargo. Whut I owe to Jess, whut I owe to my other sons, to my brothers, all the rest of the family. They would fight fer Jess, down to the last man, did I tell 'em to. But have I got the right to do hit? Even if he is my own son?"

He stood up, his weathered face mournful and perplexed beneath the heavy beard, a craggy old giant of a man, whose shoulders now were bowed with the weight of decision. "Awright," he said finally. "There's nothin' to do but put it to the family, jest like you told me. They're entitled to decide whether they want more troubles like them we run so fur to escape. They're entitled to decide whether they want to die fer Jess. They hate his guts, all of 'em, even his half brothers. But—" He squared his shoulders. "Come on," he said. "We're ridin' back to the settlement. When we git thar, the family is gonna hold a trial. We'll try Jess fer shootin' thet Ranger. Then we'll take a vote as to whether we want to turn him over to the law or go down fightin' to save him."

Followed by the men from the still, they rode back to the scattering of huts at the valley's other end. When they reached it, Canfield ordered Fargo to dismount. He gestured to the big cabin. "Go inside and wait. Ye fellers—" he addressed the men from the still "—go in thar with him and watch him. Don't let him git near no weapons. I'll round up the others."

Fargo went inside, under the muzzles of a half dozen Sharps. Bonnie was there, cooking a meal at the fireplace. Fargo sat down at the table, the others ranged around him. She turned, brought a coffee pot and cups. As she set them down, her eyes met Fargo's again. Once more, he read bad trouble in them. He turned away, and her red mouth pouted, even as she purposefully smoothed her dress more tightly over full, thrusting breasts.

The morning dragged on. One by one, two by two, Canfields clumped in, carrying rifles, hung with sixguns. They looked at Fargo strangely, aware something was up, and that he was at the center of it, but not knowing what. Young boys came in, too —and the women, but they were shooed back out again. Fargo, however, did have his first look at what the other Canfield women were like, and it was appalling. Like Indian squaws, mountaineers' women did heavy labor, men's labor, in addition to cooking, cleaning, and bearing children with the regularity of brood mares. It wore them out before their time, made crones and slatterns out of women not much more than five, ten years past Bonnie's age.

Fargo thought he understood now the desperation in her eyes. He felt a touch more sympathy for her. She was full of spirit, wildness, resisting the fate that had overtaken the others.

The men ate. They were all here now except for Roaring Tom and Jess. When they were finished, Bonnie cleared the table, then vanished, with one last searching look at Fargo. The Canfields smoked their pipes and cigars in silence, faces full of speculation. The older ones, long beards streaked with gray, were, Fargo guessed, Roaring Tom's younger brothers. On them, likely, would rest the main burden of decision.

Then the door opened and Roaring Tom and Jess entered. The younger Canfield stopped short, staring at the assembly. "What's this? What's goin' on?"

"Family council," Tom said, softly, wearily. He closed the door and shot its bolt.

"About whut?"

"About ye," Tom said. "Take off yer guns, son."

Jess's face turned red. "Take off my guns? Whut th' hell—?"

"Ye're on trial hyar."

Jess's head swiveled, as a kind of murmur ran through the room. "On trial?" he blurted. "Fer whut?"

"Fer shootin' men before they crossed our deadline. Two of Steed's riders; wuss than thet, a Texas Ranger. Ye plugged 'em without warnin' while ye was up on guard, outside the pass." The old man looked exhausted, depressed, his eyes full of grief. "Ye disobeyed my orders thet ever' man was to be challenged and turned around, if possible; thet nobody was to be feared at unless they crossed the deadline after bein' warned. And now yer disobedience has put us all in trouble along with ye. Ye know the rules, ye got to be tried fer hit, and yer punishment must be decided by the family." His voice sharpened. "So ye do whut I say. Ye take off them guns."

"I ain't takin' off anythin'!" Jess's face was pale, his eyes furious. "And I ain't standin' no trial, neither! Thet was weeks ago and you never—"

"I told ye then, ye might have to. Ye disobeyed my orders and ye know the penalty fer thet. I let it slip by, but hit cain't be put off no longer. The future of the whole family depends on hit. Now ye take them guns off, or I'll take 'em off ye myself."

Jess's lips peeled back from his teeth. He slipped into a crouch, Henry in his left hand, right dangling near his Colt. "Don't ye try it, Pappy. Don't anybody try it. Ye hear?" Then his eyes flashed, suddenly his hand went for his pistol.

Roaring Tom's arm was a blur, faster than Jess's draw. His open hand made a loud, sodden sound as, once again, he backhanded Jess. The young man's head snapped around; Tom hit him again with the other hand, at the same time seizing Jess's wrist. The Colt, half-drawn from leather, fell back into its holster and Jess howled with pain. Then Tom had snatched the Henry and jerked loose the pistol. Jess was weaponless. He stood there, face twisted in a snarl, staring at the bristling muzzles of guns that had come up to cover him.

Tom's voice was like flint on steel. "Thet's twicet ye made me hit ye, son, fer disobeyin' orders. One more time, no matter which way this comes out, ye ain't a Canfield any more and ye leave this valley on yer own and take yer chances outside." Then he turned to Rafe. "Git some rope and tie his hands, so I don't have to whup him again."

Rafe sprang up, took obvious pleasure in binding his half brother's wrists. The eyes of the other Canfields were cold while this was going on; no sympathy for Jess showed in any of them. His own gaze shuttled back and forth defiantly. His attitude was that of an enraged, cornered animal.

"Okay," Roaring Tom said. He cleared his throat. Standing beside Jess, he went on: "This hyar's a fambly trial of Jess Canfield fer disobeyin' clan orders, murderin' men· against who we had no declared blood feud, and bringin' down bad trouble on the Canfield fambly. I'm gonna tell ye whut Fargo hyar has told me. Then we'll take a vote. We'll . . . decide whut punishment Jess is to git." His voice trembled, then steadied. "Now, this hyar's the sitcheration. . . ."

He talked for a long time. He told them about the Texas Rangers. He told them about Steed's riders. And he told them of Fargo's offer to take them to the Sierra Madre. He had Fargo stand up to repeat his description of the valley.

"Steed's men I ain't skeered of," he said. "If they come atter us with guns, we got a right to shoot back, and nobody can fault us fer thet. But the Rangers is a different case. They are the law. We come out hyar because we couldn't fight the law back home. Now Jess has fixed it so we got to fight it hyar. But he is the one they want. If they git him, they won't bother the rest of usns."

He broke off. It had grown late by now; the light pouring in through the unshuttered windows was low and slanting. "So hit comes down to this," he said. "We got to decide two things. Fust, whut's to be done with Jess. Second, whether we want to move outa here into them mountains down yonder, thet air more like the ones we left back home." He paused. "Fargo hyar's come fer Jess. If we turn Jess over to him, he'll haul him outa hyar for trial and likely they'll hang him. But the Rangers won't bother us after thet. And Fargo will lead us to the Sierra Madre and settle us down thar. Er we can punish Jess on our own, the way we usually do. Banish him from the clan, er take away his guns and put him at hard labor. Er we can acquit him, let him remain a member in good standin', and ifn the Rangers come —well, then, we'll fight 'em long as we got a man can shoot."

He looked at Jess a moment, and his loud voice dropped. Now it was soft and husky. "He's my youngest boy. But he's jest tried to draw a gun on me. I . . . I can't take no part in this, nohow. Whutever y'all decide to do, I'll abide by. But I . . . cain't vote in this. Mac, I reckon ye'll hafta take it from hyar. I . . . I'm goin' outside and set until ye've decided whut Jess's fate will be."

The oldest of the brothers arose, nodding, compassion on his face. "Shore, Tom. Ye've laid it befor us fa'r and squar'. Ye go ahead. Take Fargo with ye. This is no place fer outsiders now."

Tom nodded. He drew his Colt, held it loosely at his side. "All right, Fargo. Come on."

Fargo arose, and Tom followed him out the door, closing it behind them. They moved across the settlement, and the patriarch motioned Fargo to a split-log bench in the shade of another cabin. Holding the gun steady, he sat down beside him.

"I done some hard things in my time," he said breathily, "but this is the hardest I ever done. My own son, my baby boy . . ." Then his face firmed. "But . . . there's somethin' wrong with thet younker. I don't know whut it is. There always been somethin' wrong with him. I recollect when he was little, I ketched him in the hen house one day. He had an ax in one hand, was choppin' off the heads of chickens, had done kilt half a dozen. I asked him whut the hell he was up to, he said he liked to see the way they flopped when their heads was gone." He spat into the dust. "Maybe I shoulda knowed then. Thet was ... onnatural. Maybe I did, but I closed my eyes ..."

They were silent for a while, after that. Then Fargo said, "If they vote to keep Jess in the clan, what happens to me?"

"Ye ride out through thet pass," Tom said. "When ye reach yon side, ye git yer guns back. Atter thet, ye'd better never be caught in Black Valley again. If y'are, it'll be presumed ye're huntin' Jess, and ye'll be shot on sight."

Fargo's lips thinned. That would, of course, be the next step unless—

Then the door of the big cabin swung open. The Canfield called Mac appeared there, shorter than Roaring Tom, but wide-shouldered, his beard reaching almost to his belt. "All right, Tom," he said quietly. "Ye, too, Fargo. Ye can come in now."

Roaring Tom arose as if he were stiff and sore. Heretofore, he had moved, despite his age, with a pantherish lightness, but now his shuffle was that of an old man as he crossed the dusty way between the cabins, Fargo stalking alongside. Mac stepped back to let them in.

The room was very silent, all eyes of the Canfields on Roaring Tom. Jess, hands still tied behind his back, stood straight, eyes glittering as they met Fargo's. His mouth curled in a strange, confident grimace that could only be called a sneer.

Mac Canfield shut the door behind them. He moved to the center of the room. "Tom, we voted. And the vote was a hunderd per cent. And this is whut we've decided." He cleared his throat.

"Fust of all, thet valley down in Mexico sounds mighty good to us. This ain't never been like home hyar. Not enough timber, too damned hot, cactus instid of laurel and rhododendron. All of us, we're homesick fer some real, man-sized mountains. We have voted u-nanimously, thet we'd like to pull out fer Mexico."

Tom let out a long breath, realizing that he had just heard a death sentence pronounced on his son.

Mac raised his hand before the old man could speak. "Jess," he said, "has jest about forfeited all right to be a Canfield. Bushwhackin' a Whipple's one thing; drawin' down on a stranger and shootin' him through the back's another. Thet's murder. *But—*" His blue eyes lanced toward Fargo. "But the Canfields have never turned none of their kin over to the law to go to jail, and they ain't gonna do hit now. No Canfield's gonna be locked in no cage and then hanged like a rabbit in a snare. So we decided thet Fargo cain't take him outa here to put him in no jailhouse."

"Thank God," whispered Roaring Tom.

"So hit's up to Fargo," Mac said. "If he wants Jess, he's got to take him, man-to-man. They kin fight, anyway they please—trial by combat, like we used to call hit. Jess gits to choose the weapons. This fight will be to the death . . ."

"Oh," Tom said gustily. He looked at Fargo.

"If Fargo's man enough to take him, he can have him. If Jess takes Fargo, he rides clear of us Canfields and never comes back. If Fargo kills Jess, he's got to take us to the Sierra Madre. If Jess kills him, we'll tough hit out here as best we kin. Thet's the way we got hit figgered; thet's the way hit's gonna be. Unless Fargo don't want to fight. In thet case, he rides out now and never comes back. After which,

113

tomorrow, Jess rides out the same way. Either one of 'em try to return he'll be shot on sight."

He looked at Fargo. "Whut do you say, man? You want Jess bad enough to fight him to git him?"

Fargo turned toward Jess. He saw the grin on the bound man's countenance, the utter surety, the confidence. "Yeah," he said. "I want him that bad."

Mac turned to Jess. "Ye?"

"After I kill him, I go," Jess said. "And the rest of ye, all of ye, can go to hell." His eyes shuttled to Roaring Tom. "Ye too, old man, damn ye."

Tom let out that gusty breath again. He drew himself up. "So be it," he said. "Cut him loose and let him choose his weapons."

Jess's gaze met Fargo's again; and in that instant it flashed into Fargo's mind what weapons Jess would choose. He had beaten Jess with his fists and, this morning, at shooting. He was not surprised when, Jess, hands freed, rubbed his wrists and said, tersely, "Knives." Then he reached out and whisked the huge Bowie off his father's hip.

Chapter VII

"All right," Fargo said. "I want my own knife."

"Git it fer him," Tom said heavily.

Fargo's weapons were still in the corner, where Tom had piled them the night before. Mac went to them, brought back the Batangas knife. Jess made passes with the heavy Bowie. His lip curled at the sight of the blade from the Philippines, two inches shorter and much lighter than his weapon, as Fargo snapped back the folded handles.

"You aim to come up against me with thet knittin' needle?" He sliced the air with the big Bowie blade.

"I figure on it," Fargo said, and made a couple of limbering passes.

"Outside," Mac said. "Past the settlement. Out in the open, whar thar's plenty room." He tilted up the muzzle of a Sharps. "Nobody tries to cut until I give the word. Fust one to take unfa'r advantage, he gits a rifle ball."

They stalked out, Jess in the lead, still flexing his wrists. Fargo followed, doing the same. Roaring Tom was the last in line. They crossed the settlement, reached the open ground beyond. There was another hour of light, Fargo figured. Before the sun went down, either he or Jess would be dead.

On a flat tufted with grama grass, the Canfields made a spacious ring around them. The children had come up to watch too, fascinated and wide-eyed. Fargo and Jess stood inside the ring, stripped to the waist, knives down, facing one another. The evening light glinted off of bronzed, muscular torsos.

Jess's face was confident. "Three y'ars ago," he said thinly, "afore we left the Smokies, two Whipples come at me with knives. I gutted both of 'em and they never laid an edge on me."

"Good for you," said Fargo quietly.

"Enough talk," Mac said. "Ye two ready?"

Fargo looked around the ring. Roaring Tom was nowhere to be seen.

"I'm ready," he said.

"Me, too," Jess said.

"Then cut loose your wolves," said Mac. "Go to hit."

The blades came up, glinting in the slanting light.

The two men moved cautiously toward one another, circling, appraising, each getting the measure of his opponent. Fargo was not thinking now; thinking was fatal in a knife-fight. A knife-fight was all speed and reflex. Once you were in it, your body, your nerves and muscles, had to take over. Brain was a handicap. It made you guess what the other man would do, and if you were wrong, you were finished. Better to depend on skill, instinct.

Instinct told Fargo now that he was up against a

118

man with a natural talent, maybe even genius, as a knife-fighter, and plenty of acquired skill on top of that. Jess's movements were sleek and easy and free-flowing as those of a panther as he circled Fargo, sizing up the older man's guard. He was not one whit less coldblooded or determined than his opponent. This was, perhaps, going to be as tough a fight with blades as Fargo had ever been in. Suddenly he made up his mind to carry the fight to Jess and went in quickly—crouched, shoulder out, shielding heart and gut with that and his folded left arm, his blade darting like a snake's tongue.

It rang on the steel of the heavy Bowie, as Jess parried deftly, and slid aside under the big knife's weight. Then, as Fargo whirled, Jess thrust, and only Fargo's quick, instinctive turn kept him from being split. The Bowie's long, glittering blade thrust between his arm and body, ripping skin on his flank as it touched him when Jess pulled back. Then they circled one another again, each seeking an opening.

Jess charged next. He came in with the blade swooping, swirling, darting, menacing, seeking to pull Fargo's away and make an opening. Fargo gave him none, and when the Bowie slashed for his belly he fended it with all the strength in his right arm. Steel chimed on steel, slid off, and they backed away once more. Then Fargo moved in.

The long, thin blade of the Batangas knife winked out, sheered off the Bowie, drew back. Jess took that instant when Fargo was slightly off balance and ran in, not thrusting but hacking, seeking with the chopping weight of the big weapon to sever the tendons in Fargo's wrist. Fargo jerked his body, dropped his right arm as his knife winked in the air. He caught the knife in his left—the equivalent of the border shift quick transfer as it was performed with a sixgun–and came in from the other flank.

119

This was a tactic he'd often used, taking advantage of being ambidextrous, but this time he'd miscalculated. Jess had not forgotten how Fargo had shifted balance in the fistfight at Fort Davis, and had been waiting for the move. He took advantage of the opening, slashed in, and suddenly blood coursed hot and streaming down Fargo's flank; the grate of steel on bone sounded in his ear. Only the rib the Bowie's edge encountered saved Fargo. But now Fargo knew his time was running out. This slice would bleed a lot and weaken him; he had no more than three or four minutes left before his strength would begin to fade.

Fargo bared his teeth in a wolfish snarl. He forgot all science, all calculation. A kind of red mist swirled before his eyes as he felt blood flowing down his waist, his leg. Suddenly he blurred in, light on his feet, using boxer's footwork, and the Batangas knife chopped and thrust and chopped and thrust and chopped again. Jess parried deftly, coolly, but the raging ferocity of Fargo's attack drove him back and around the circle and still Fargo came on, thrusting, chopping, seeking an opening. In the slanting light, the evening hush, the blades shone and rang, chiming like bells, again and again; and Fargo pressed on mercilessly. He was not thinking about himself now, not thinking about defense; all he wanted to do was get past Jess's guard one time, only once, and kill the man. In that instant there was no more reason or humanity in him than a charging bull, and not much more caution.

One way or the other, this had to be ended quickly; he had to kill Jess within the next two minutes or become vulnerable from loss of blood and die himself.

The sudden change in attitude from coolness to ferocity dismayed Canfield. He swung, tried to get distance between them, but Fargo would not let him and came on savagely, working in ever closer. Through sweat that veiled his own eyes, Fargo saw perspiration running down Jess's face as the man parried every thrust. Jess's face was almost bloodless now, too; he must never have met a man who came in so viciously, with such skill and yet with such disregard for his own safety. There was something awesome, frightening, about Fargo's fury and desperation. It shook Jess up; and suddenly he lost his self-possession and his coolness. He began to flail and parry more wildly, more desperately, as he saw the madness in Fargo's eye. He began to back more swiftly; now he was on the run. Red and slippery with blood, Fargo came in relentlessly, as remorseless as death itself. His blade was never still, always flicking, darting, hacking, seeking an opening through which he could deliver a killing stab.

For all his skill, for all his genius, this was what Jess lacked: the ability to forget himself and his safety to embrace death if, in dying, he could bring down his opponent. In this instant, he must have seen in Fargo the Grim Reaper embodied, using a foreign knife instead of a scythe, and it broke his nerve. Fargo heard his stertorous breathing, saw fear and dismay in his eyes. Now he knew that panic had seeped into Jess and would make him over-react; and if he were to win, Fargo had to make that panic grow, that awed fear at facing an opponent who was not a human being so much as a force of nature. Fargo's lips peeled back from his teeth in a snarl totally feral, and without thinking of his own safety, he bore in even harder. Jess tried to back-pedal, tossing his head to clear his eyes of sweat and downfalling locks of tow-colored hair. Then, in a crucial peak of panic, he sought to gamble all on one last chance and came back at Fargo almost blindly, no longer thrusting but hacking madly with the heavy Bowie, determined to use it to knock Fargo's lighter knife aside and chop Fargo to shreds with it.

That was what Fargo wanted. He did not calculate; all his moves were rage-born and instinctive, but Jess's response and new tactics gave him his chance. Fargo lowered his guard, presented himself almost naked to Jess's charge. Jess came in with the Bowie raised for a blow that would cut Fargo's throat. There was fear and determination in his racked, grim expression. The Bowie whistled down and sideways. Fargo fell, ducked, heard the knife rush through the short white hair that clad his scalp. He then came up from a half-kneeling posture inside Jess's guard and caught Jess below the navel, thrust in and ripped upward even as he shoved forward.

Jess screamed.

Fargo felt the Bowie slide down his back, having dropped from Jess's strengthless hand. He turned his own blade, pulled up until bone caught it, then stepped back, feeling only exultance and a wild and dizzy weakness.

Jess was red all across his front. His hands clasped over the ripped belly, holding his entrails in. He stared down at his own death-wound with terrified, slowly comprehending eyes.

Then a voice rang out, a great bellow. "For God's sake, Fargo! Kill him! Kill the boy!"

It was Roaring Tom. He had stepped from behind a cabin at the edge of the settlement. So, Fargo thought blurrily, he had not been able to resist watching after all. The wound Fargo had dealt his son was one that Roaring Tom knew was agonizing, and that the agony would go on and on for it would take Jess a long time to die.

And then Fargo moved. It was all he could do for

the grief-stricken old man whom he admired. He moved in and his blade went out and Jess saw it come—his eyes widened, and he grunted as the steel pierced his heart; then he dropped, quickly, inertly, dead before he hit the ground.

A sigh went up from the crowd. Fargo heard somebody crying, sobbing. At first he thought it must be a woman who had dared to join the on-lookers. But then, through sweat-burning eyes, he saw the source of the sound. Roaring Tom lurched through the crowd, stood there crying above the body of his dead son. His hand was on his pistol's butt. He half drew the Navy Colt as he whirled on Fargo, face contorted. Fargo stood there weakly, dizzy from loss of blood. He could not even raise the knife again.

Then Roaring Tom let the Colt drop back into leather. He took his hand away. His voice was a croak. "All right, Fargo," he gasped. "Ye won fa'r and squar'. I hope ye're satisfied. I hope the Rangers are. My youngest son is dead." He made a strange, sad gesture, tears streaming down the leathery cheeks and soaking his beard. "Someboy patch him up afore he bleeds to death hisself. Where's Bonnie? She's good at thet. Git Bonnie." Then he turned away and stalked through the crowd and walked far out on the basin's floor, his figure growing smaller and smaller, until it finally disappeared in a swale.

Mac moved up beside Fargo, took his arm.

"Come inside," he said, not unkindly. "Bonnie will patch ye up." And he stripped off his own shirt and pressed it against Fargo's bleeding flank.

He was drunk, roaring drunk.

It was the only anesthesia the Canfields had— Canfield corn. Bonnie had made him drink half a pint of it, before she began to stitch up the gaping edges of the cleansed wound. Since Canfield liquor was probably well over a hundred proof, and since he had swilled the whole half pint hot, unmixed, and in about ten minutes, Fargo, who could hold a quart of ordinary whiskey without becoming tanglefooted, felt it profoundly. Stretched out on the board table in the big room of the cabin, he was hardly aware of the needle's prick.

He felt a curious mixture of sadness and exultance. He was glad that he'd killed Jess, but sorry that Jess was Tom Canfield's son. Anyhow, he'd done the best he could, finished the boy off quickly. If Jess had gutted him, he would probably have stood over Fargo's twitching body and laughed and let him take his time dying.

Then, from far away, he heard Bonnie say, commandingly, "Some of you carry him to the lean-to."

Next, he was on the cot in what had been the jail. Vaguely, he was aware that Bonnie was beside him; her voice still seemed distant. "Y'all git out, now. I'll sit up with him and see to him." He heard the others leave and was aware that she had closed the door.

He slept.

When he awakened, the room was dark. He lay there for a while, the hangover worse than the pain in his side. It took some moments for everything that had happened to come back. Then he tried to sit up.

A small hand against his muscle-banded chest pushed him back.

"Lay down. Ye're hurt."

Fargo lay back. "Not bad," he said. "I been hurt worse than this."

"Then ye must be made of arn," said Bonnie's voice.

"I've been hurt worse than this and fought on all day in battles," he said. "I'd like a drink of water."

"Here." He heard the clink of dipper in bucket. Then her hand moved behind his head, propping it. Cool water touched his lips; he drank long and thirstily.

"That's better," he said. "Any whiskey here?"

"Yeah. I figured ye'd need it."

"Not for the wound," he said. "That's nothing. For this damn-blasted hangover."

She passed him a fruit jar. He drank, and she gave him the dipper to chase it with. His soul came back into his body and he was all right; he was fine. His heavily bandaged side burned, but he could ignore that. He had trained himself to feel no self-pity when he was hurt, and most of the pain of any wound came from self-pity and fright.

"I'm okay, now," he said, sitting up stiffly. "What time is it?" Before she could answer, he thumbed a gold-cased railroad watch, remorselessly accurate, from his pants, struck a match, stared at it. Midnight. "You been here with me all this time?" he asked.

Bonnie's face was pale in the match flame; it struck golden glints from her tawny hair. "Yeah," she said. "I been watchin' over ye."

"Thanks," Fargo said softly.

"Except fer the guards up on the rim," she whispered, "ever'body else's in bed. Even Pappy."

"Tom," said Fargo. "How's he taking it?"

"Not so hard," she said. "Kind of relieved. If ye hadn't did hit, he would have had to do hit sooner or later hisself. He said thet tonight at supper. Jess kept buckin' him, Jess was crazy, he woulda killed Pappy soon as anybody else. Pappy knows thet."

Fargo lay back. There was silence for a moment. Then Bonnie said, "Are ye strong enough to talk, now?"

"Sure," said Fargo.

Her hand closed around his. "Fargo, ye got to help me."

"Help you, how?"

"Git outa here." Her voice shook. "Git away from the Canfields."

"Huh?"

"I got to." Her tone was vibrant, intense. "Especially afore ye take 'em down to Mexico! When they git down thar, they're buried, forever. Thet's whut they want, the rest of 'em! But hit ain't whut I want! Because, you don't know whut hit's like to be a Canfield woman."

Fargo said nothing.

"I got to find some way out. If I don't, I'll be forced to marry my first cousin I cain't stand the sight of, spend the resta my life a slave like all the other women . . . spinnin', weavin', choppin' wood, cookin', haulin' water, birthin' a baby ever' ten months . . . I'll be an ole woman by the time I'm thutty. Ye seen my mama in Fort Davis."

"Yes," Fargo said, remembering the withered crone who had looked to be seventy, maybe older.

"She died this month. She warn't but forty, but she was plumb wore out. Ye seen how she looked, birthed Jess at seventeen, me at twenty-two . . . And all thet hard work . . . I won't end up like thet, I won't. Fargo, ye got to help me! When she died, I made up my mind. I ain't gonna go like her. And if ye take 'em all to Mexico, this is my last chance to excape."

Then, suddenly, her breasts were pushing against his naked chest, her lips close to his. "I got no money to pay ye with," she whispered, "but I got myself. Ever' since I seen ye in Fort Davis, I wanted to . . . If ye would help me, I would be good to ye, I would do anything ye wanted to, anything . . ."

Her hand roamed over his body. The whiskey

126

burning in him made him even more responsive than he might have been. Incautious, too. "I know yer hurt too bad now," she whispered.

"Who says I am?" he heard himself answer.

"Ye'd open up that wound—"

"Not if you stitched it tight."

She was silent for a moment. Then she said, "I may not be much, but I'm an expert seamstress." And he heard the rustle of clothes in darkness.

Then her body was on the bed beside him, her hands fumbling with buttons and belt. "Fargo," she whispered.

After that, nobody talked for a long time.

Somewhat later, she said, "Ye *will* help me?"

Fargo lay silently, smoking, looking up into darkness. His mind was working swiftly. "Yes," he said, having figured out a use for her. "Yes, I'll help you."

She let out a gusty breath of gratification. She pressed soft, naked breasts more tightly against him, shivered as his hand caressed the smooth curve of buttock and hip.

"Get up," said Fargo. "Get up, get dressed and find my gear. Rafe brought in my gear, didn't he?"

"Yes."

"Bring me my binoculars case."

She vanished. Four, five minutes later, she returned. "Here."

He opened the case, took out the glasses. Then his hand unlatched the false bottom. He slipped four bills from the wad of money crammed in there. "Here," he said, passing them to her. "Four hundred dollars."

"Good Lord!" Her gasp was full of awe. Probably she had never held above a dollar in her hand in her whole life.

"That will keep you for six months in El Paso, if

you're careful," Fargo said. "Go to the Regal Hotel, down on The Alameda. If things break right and you care to wait, I'll be there in about three months. Don't gamble and don't get mixed up with other men and don't give anybody a dime unless you get value received and don't go hog wild on fancy clothes. When I git there, I'll see you get all the fancy clothes you need. You understand?"

"I understand," she whispered.

"Don't let anybody con you into a whorehouse. There are a lot of people in El Paso who make their living as crimps. They make white slaves out of girls. Don't talk to strange men." He grinned in the darkness; it sounded as if he were giving a Sunday school lecture. But she was *damned* naive.

"I understand all thet," she whispered. "I'll do whut ye say. But—"

"But you've got to earn that money. Do you know where Jim Hanna's Oxbow headquarters are?"

"Hanna? Yes, I know thet place."

"All right. When the time comes, and it ain't now, I'll mount you on my sorrel. When I give you the word, you ride hell for leather for Hanna's Oxbow. Tell him to move his cattle. You understand? That's all you got to tell him—that Fargo said to move his cattle. Then you go on to El Paso."

"I understand," she whispered.

"All right. Hide the money, get your traps ready to leave at any time, and wait. I'll let you know when. Likely it will be right after we fight Steed."

"What?"

"Never mind," he said. "Go on, now. I'm all right. You go on and let me sleep. I'll meet you in El Paso later on."

"All right," she whispered. Her lips pressed against his. He heard the rustle as, in darkness, she

128

dressed. Then she went out and closed the door. Fargo grinned at nothing and lay back, drunk and drained; and then he slept.

Chapter VIII

Now that he had his guns back, he felt whole and complete again. The Fox sawed-off muzzles hung down behind his shoulder, his Colt and knife were in their sheaths, the Winchester in its boot, and his bandoliers crisscrossed over his torso, as he and Roaring Tom together rode the high rimrock on big Canfield mules.

The morning after his fight with Jess—two days ago—he had stiffly entered the front room of the big cabin. Roaring Tom, haggard and pouch-eyed, had sat at the table, loading shotgun shells. He looked up at the man who had killed his son.

Fargo stood tensely as their eyes met. He was unarmed, but the old man had his Navy Colt and squirrel gun on the bench beside him.

Then Roaring Tom said, heavily, "All right, Fargo. Come in, set. Bonnie will bring ye breakfast."

Fargo cautiously sat down opposite the old man. Spread before Tom were nine buckshot, lined up like beads. Each had been split open with a sharp knife. Now Canfield picked up a coil of thin, bronze piano wire, snipped off nearly a yard. "We buried Jess late last night," he said.

Fargo did not answer.

"Better ye killed him than I had to," Roaring Tom went on. "And I woulda, sooner or later. He was like a dawg gone mad, ready to bite even his own kin." He lined up the split shot, pressed the length of wire into them, linking them together like a necklace.

"I have seen my pappy, my brothers, others of my sons killed in the feud back home," Tom said. "I thought I had burnt out all the grievin' in me. But thar was some left. Last night, hit burnt out, too." With the butt of the Bowie, he hammered the split shot closed, clamping them on the wire. He picked up the whole assembly, coiled it down into a shotgun shell, carefully. "Now, I'm ready to go to Mexico. And fight, if thet's whut hit takes to git thar." He looked at Fargo. "Ever seed a man hit with a rig like this?"

"No," said Fargo.

"We load shells like thet back whar I come from. If jest one shot hits a man, they all whup around and git him. And the wire itself—hit cuts like a knife. Hit a man squar' with this, he'll look like he walked into a sawmill blade." He crimped the shell, set it aside. "Thet's fifty of 'em I made this mornin', waitin' fer Steed's men to come."

"They'll come," Fargo said.

"I hope we'll be gone afore they do. I got men dismantlin' the still, loadin' the wagons, roundin' up the livestock now. But ye don't move a clan this size overnight. Hit'll take three days, four, anyhow, to git ready to go. Meanwhile, if Steed's gunmen come, ye reckon they'll be satisfied to know we're leavin'? Let us out without a fight?"

"No," said Fargo. "That's not Steed's way—nor Lin Gordon's, who's leading 'em."

"Nor ours, either, fer thet matter," Tom said. "Personal, I'd like to git out of hyar without no more bloodshed. But the boys are tetchy. We Canfields are tired o' bein' pursecuted and run from pillar to post. Likely thar would be fightin' anyway. Somebody would tetch hit off. Ye—" He picked up another shell. "Ye're honor bound to be on our side."

"I am," Fargo said. "I want to see Steed whipped and I want to see him whipped good. His gunmen wiped out so he can't raise another batch. Not just chased away, but—eliminated."

"If they come atter us, we aim to do thet. Our patience is plumb wore out. The question is, how?" He dropped nine loose buckshot in the shell. Then picked up a canister, poured a stream of smaller shot, birdshot, in after them. The tiny pellets filled every crevice between the larger slugs, packed the shell solid with extra lead, extra killing power. Fargo's mouth quirked in admiration. These Canfields knew every trick in the book.

"Hit's gonna be rough," Tom went on. "Ye said there'd likely be fifty of them. There ain't but thirty, twenty-nine, now of us. We're gonna . . . miss Jess. In a dust-up like thet, he was good as any other five men I got."

"I'll try to take his place," Fargo said. "Can I have my guns back?"

"In the corner; help ye'self." Tom went on filling shells. Fargo got his weapons, came back to the bench. There were empty loops in the shotgun-ammo bandolier. He looked at Tom and the old man nodded. Fargo selected enough of the piano-wire chain shot and the other to fill them.

"There's one thing, though, Tom," he said. "This

135

fight, if there is one, has to take place *inside* the valley."

Roaring Tom stared. "Whut? Thet's throwin' away the only advantage we got. The high rimrock up thar, whar we kin shoot down. Thirty men, mostly armed with singleshot guns, cain't stand against fifty professionals with repeatin' rifles if we give up thet advantage."

"You'll have to, though. Steed draws a lot of water in this country. This fight is going to have to be clearcut self-defense. Lin Gordon and his men are gonna have to attack and shoot first and the battle is gonna have to take place in here, on land that you claim. If you snipe 'em while they're outside the valley, Steed will holler murder and have you so tied up in courts and law and jails that you'll never get to Mexico. If the fight's in here, where those men had no business being, I can round up enough force" —he was thinking of Tom Hanna— "to offset Steed, keep you clear of the law." Bonnie appeared then, looked at him and smiled. He did not smile back as she went to the fireplace, began to cook his breakfast.

"Keepin' cl'ar of the law's one thing," Tom said. "But hit don't help dead men. I let Steed's gunnies in this valley, we'll lose half our clan. Thet ain't my aim. I want to take this whole fambly to Mexico."

Fargo grinned, coldly and with a certain happiness at the prospect of what lay ahead. "You'll get 'em all there, if you'll listen to me. I know Lin Gordon of old and what he'll do—the same thing I would if I was in his shoes and didn't know you were expecting me. And don't worry about being outnumbered. You've got reinforcements right here in the valley you haven't even used yet. Good fighters, and they'll make the difference."

Canfield stared, blinked. "Thet knife wound must

have got to you. I know how many fightin' men I got."

"I didn't say anything about fighting *men*," Fargo said, still grinning. "Let me have some breakfast, and then I'll tell you what we'll do."

Now, on the high rim, Fargo reined in his mule, lifted his field glasses. He surveyed the valley outside the wall of the rock, across which Gordon must approach. Nothing showed, nothing moved. Fargo had not expected anything to. Gordon would come at night.

He turned in the saddle; through the glasses, the settlement below, loaded wagons parked within it, loomed large. He grinned faintly; his sorrel was saddled, tethered outside the big cabin. When the time came, Bonnie could get to it without trouble.

She had come to the lean-to again last night. He had been sober and in good shape, and had taken what she offered him without reservation. He then had repeated his instructions and received again her promise to carry them out.

He pouched the glasses, squinted at the sun. An hour's light left. His hand stroked the shotgun sling. They would come tonight. Somehow he knew it; he could smell it in the air, the way a wild animal could smell an approaching storm long before it hit.

"There's nothing out there now," he said. "But after dark, there will be. Let's move along and check everything out."

They rode the high rim, headed north to where it merged with a mountain peak. When the mountainside towered above them, too steep even for mules, they tethered the animals in one of the clumps of juniper that made superb cover all along the inner slope of the barrier. Gunmen could hole up in those juniper thickets and using smokeless powder rain

137

fire on the settlement below and remain wholly invisible. Such positions were the ones Gordon would seek out for his men, the ones Fargo wanted him to have.

Canfield looked at the juniper dubiously. "I still say, you git men in them thickets, they're gonna be powerful hard to find."

Fargo grinned. "No harder than bears or panthers in those laurel hells up in the smokies."

Tom was serious; then he grinned, too. "Maybe ye're right. Maybe we'll have us one good hunt, anyhow, before we head for the border."

On foot, they edged around the hump of the mountain. On his first morning in Black Valley, Fargo had spotted the deep draw that cut across it. Part of his trade was reading, learning terrain and turning it to his advantage. Now, when he and Tom entered it, they found it full of Canfield men, armed to the teeth. The barrels of long muzzle-loading rifles glinted in the dying sun; the bandoliers of cartridges for the Sharps buffalo guns winked brassily and clicked with every movement. So did the belts of the shotgun shells, for the big twelve and ten-gauge hammerguns they carried. Except for the four on guard duty at the pass, every Canfield fighting man over the age of fifteen was here.

"Fargo says they'll come tonight," Roaring Tom announced. "Everybody ready hyar?"

"Ready, brother," answered Mac, in charge of this detail. The muted whining of many dogs was background to their conversation. Further up the draw, the Canfield hounds, two dozen enormous, cold-jawed brutes, strained at leashes, unable to bay their impatience because of the rawhide thongs tied around their muzzles to silence them. Tom grinned as he and Fargo walked among them. "Thar's three things a Canfield dog will purely eat alive. Bears,

138

wildcats and strangers. Hit's a good thing ye're wearin' them ole clothes of mine thet smell like me, Fargo, or they'd bust them muzzle-strings to git thar teeth in ye."

"That's why I asked you for them," Fargo said. He kept moving among the dogs, letting their scent rub off on him, fondling them, talking to them softly, making sure that all knew him.

"Well, if ye're sure they'll come this evenin', I reckon we might as well stay up hyar with the rest." Roaring Tom sat down, looked to his weapons: the squirrel gun, a shotgun slung over his shoulder, the Navy Colt. Mac came to hunker on his heels beside Fargo and his older brother.

"Let me see if I got this straight. Thar'll be shootin' at the pass tonight. But we don't do nothin' about thet. We jest set tight all night and wait 'til daybreak. When dawn comes, we're to be all spread out up thar—" He gestured to the slope just below the rim. "But we don't take our positions 'til an hour before daylight. Then, when Gordon's men open up on the settlement, thet's when we cut loose our wolf."

Fargo grinned coldly. "Not your wolf. Your hounds."

Mac answered him with another grin. "By God, if this works, hit's the slickest trick I ever heerd of. Hit'll be better'n a b'ar hunt and a turkey shoot put together."

"Just remember," Fargo said, "once it gets dark, everybody's got to be dead quiet. The whole thing has to be carried out in absolute silence. You bush-whackers ought to know how to take your positions without even making a rock roll."

Roaring Tom spat. "Ain't a man hyar ain't learned how to move through mountains like fog hitself. Thar ain't no room fer noise when ye're huntin' squirrels in the big timber—or stalkin' or bein' stalked by another fambly in a blood feud."

Fargo leaned back against a rock. "Then let's get some sleep," he said.

He closed his eyes. He was gambling everything on being right. But there was no worry in him, no fear that he was wrong. He knew Lin Gordon, and how Gordon would come at the Canfields; and Gordon did not know he was here with that knowledge.

He slept and then awakened for a supper of dried meat and water and a swig or two of Canfield corn. He went to sleep again until the gunfire from the pass awakened him at nearly midnight.

It exploded in a sudden roar, from the hills above and the outside valley floor below. Even from this distance, two miles away, the flashes were visible in the clear night air. It sounded as if more men were firing than really were. The Canfields on the rim had instructions to use what repeating weapons were available in the clan's armory and to keep the bullets flying. Gordon's men, creating a diversion before the pass to draw Canfield guards off, would be using the same tactics, simulating an attack in force.

Fargo sat up tensely. But Gordon would be too wise to concentrate his main attack on the pass. A handful of defenders up there could mow down his men like wheat. He would do what Fargo had done —the unexpected: move the bulk of his forces across the valley on foot, climb the wall far from the pass, where its slope gentled, cross the rim in darkness, come down the other side while the Canfields were distracted by the diversion, and take cover in the juniper, within fair rifle range of the settlement below. He would pour a terrific fire into those cabins down there, with little fear of retaliation, of being seen in the superb cover of the juniper thickets. When the defending force had been softened up, he would make his charge. Fargo's lips peeled back as the shooting at the pass intensified, ebbed, roared again. Everything was going according to plan. If only he could hold the Canfields back until just before dawn.

Because they were restless, itching for a fight, itching to run to the sound of the guns. They seemed to plunge against invisible tethers, eager for battle, like the big hounds in the draw above that plunged against their real tethers. Fargo, Tom and Mac moved among the men, sternly warning them to silence and to patience.

The shooting at the pass went on a long time, then dwindled to a crackle and ebbed entirely.

"That means they're over the rim, now," Fargo whispered to Tom. "Gordon's bunch at the pass has done its job, pulled back. They'll want you people to think they're whipped, giving up. Tomorrow, when the real fight starts, they'll try to come through again. Your men up there know to let 'em, don't they?"

"I've drilled 'em all in yer plan, over and over," Tom said. He looked at the stars. "Damn, hit's a long time to day."

It did seem so. Even Fargo was restless, knowing that the juniper thickets down there on the valley's inside slope were crawling with Lin Gordon's armed men. And Lin himself, he thought eagerly, would be in there somewhere. Maybe this time they would find out which one was best . . .

Everything was graveyard still. Then, down in the settlement, a Canfield rooster crowed.

Tom and Mac looked at Fargo.

Fargo nodded. "Now," he said.

The men stirred, making hardly any sound. The

141

big dogs were untied, taken in hand, each man holding one on a leash. From the draw, the Canfields, with Fargo in the lead, fanned out around the mountain and then to the rimrock, keeping just below its edge lest they skyline themselves and give their plan away.

Fargo marveled at their skill and silence as the mountaineers dispersed themselves. Thirty men, drifting like fog across the slopes. Moving in behind Gordon's men, who would be farther down in the brush, setting the trap that would be sprung at daylight. If, Fargo thought . . . if everything went according to plan.

He himself made no sound as he moved Indian fashion across the slope. He found position in a fragrant juniper thicket exactly halfway between the pass and the mountain. Roaring Tom, holding a huge black hound on tight leash, moved in beside him. Fargo had already put a round into the Winchester; now he pulled back its hammer to full cock.

Tom kept the dog tight-gathered, one arm around its neck, a big hand on its muzzle-thongs, the loaded squirrel gun across his knees, powder horn and shot pouch at hand, the steerhorn trumpet close by.

The sky began to gray. Night peeled back from the slope below; the rising sun flooded it with tentative light. The clumps of juniper swam into definition; silent, apparently uninhabited, not a target showing in any of them. Nor would there be; Gordon's men would know how to use their cover to the best advantage.

The light moved down the valley wall. Now the settlement came into view. Roosters were crowing, their clarion sounds echoing from mountainside to mountainside. Nothing stirred on the slope below, no sign of life revealed itself.

And then, like the breaking of a sudden storm,

gunfire erupted from the juniper below them, across a wide front, all aimed at the cluster of cabins on the valley floor. Fargo grinned. He'd been right. Gordon's men were there, okay! They'd infiltrated under cover of darkness, taken up their positions and—

The roar of shooting was thunderous as a tremendous rain of fire was poured down the valley by Gordon's force. Still, Fargo held a restraining hand on Tom's shoulder. Then the counterfire came, white smoke blossoming from slits and firing ports, as the women and children barricaded in the cabin followed Fargo's instructions. They sent a hail of lead back up the slope, but they deliberately shot low, taking no chances of hitting their own men higher up.

To Gordon, though, it must have looked as if all the Canfield fighting men were in that house, returning fire. His force's attention would be riveted on it, now—any thought of surprise from behind erased.

And so it was time. Fargo looked at Roaring Tom. "Cut loose your hound," he said.

Tom picked up the steerhorn trumpet. He blew a long, winding note that rang above the gunfire. Then, quickly, deftly, he whipped the muzzle thongs loose from the big dog's jaws. It snarled; Tom slipped its leash.

Like a rocket, an arrow loosed from a bow, it shot out of the juniper thicket and bounded down the hill, savage from confinement and restraint. And on the steerhorn's signal, twenty-three more just like it broke from cover, the scent of strangers already strong and infuriating in their nostrils. The whole pack coursed down the slope, and suddenly the valley rang with their hollow, bell-like baying. Black and tan and big as yearling calves, they flashed down the hill, eating up the distance with long legs moving so fast they were a blur. Their keen noses guided them; before Gordon's men knew what was happening, the great dogs were on them in the thickets.

The barrage of firing slackened. Suddenly there was yelling, mingled with snarls and howls and roars. There was also the cough of handguns, the yelp of wounded dogs.

Fargo had kept his eyes on the dog Roaring Tom unleashed. In seconds it had covered two hundred yards, three, four. Then it disappeared in a clump of juniper, and like bears breaking cover, the gunmen who hid in it were suddenly visible as they were attacked without warning by a hundred pounds of snarling hound and sought to fight it off. A red shirt flashed among the trees; Fargo, ready, snapped off a shot with the Winchester. He heard a man scream, and then another broke from cover and ran low across the slope with the dog ravening at his heels. Roaring Tom yelled something, a kind of a war cry, raised the squirrel rifle, tracked the gunman for two seconds. Then the old rifle thundered, powdersmoke obscured vision; when it cleared, the man lay sprawled, while the dog worried his body savagely for an instant and then bounded on.

And that was the way it was happening all across the slope. The hounds went surely, accurately, to each clump of cover in which gunmen were hidden. Not even the most seasoned fighting man could lie still to ward off such an assault; Gordon's crew, in singles, twos and threes, sprang to their feet to combat the dogs. And when they did, the sharpshooters on the hill, men used to dropping squirrel-sized targets with one well-aimed shot, took them. All along the slope, muzzle-loaders and Sharps coughed and roared. A huge fog of white powdersmoke rolled down the hill, making an effective screen.

Roaring Tom had reloaded his long rifle with

dazzling speed; the dog had left the corpse, it ran, and flushed out another gunman. A man in a khaki shirt sprang from a swale in which he'd taken shelter, the dog ripping at his left sleeve. Oblivious to the rifle fire above, he drew a Colt automatic, put it to the hound's head, pulled the trigger. The dog fell, dead at once. It was the last shot the khaki-shirted man ever fired. Roaring Tom dropped him with a rifle ball through the head, and his body slumped across the dog.

Other hounds were dying, as Gordon's men, recovering from surprise, fought back. But the big dogs were tricky targets, bounding and dodging; and more of the gunmen's shots missed than hit.

But the mountain men did not miss; nor did Fargo. The hillside below swarmed with targets, now, and Fargo grinned, levering round after round into his Winchester, firing, finding another target, firing again. The screams of dying men and moans of wounded dogs mingled with the howling, baying and snarling of the undaunted, maddened bear hounds still alive and the shouts and yells of their victims. And still the muzzle-loaders and Sharps did their deadly work.

Now, thought Fargo, it was time. He nudged Roaring Tom, sprang to his feet, slung the Winchester. He whipped the shotgun loose, thumbed extra rounds from his bandolier. Roaring Tom scrambled up, discarded the squirrel rifle for an ancient double-barreled twelve-gauge. He raised his trumpet to his lips, blew three short bursts. Then, at his signal, the hill men charged.

They poured down the slope with shotguns and pistols, and they sent before them a deadly rain of lead. Buckshot raked the juniper clumps; sought running men who broke cover, trying to escape. As they closed the range, the fire increased. Now, demoralized, Gordon's men broke, ran down the hill.

Then a voice rose above the melee—one Fargo recognized. "Damn it, turn and fight! It's your only chance! Stand fast and fight!" Fargo swung his head just in time to see Lin Gordon, crouching in a nest of boulders, pop back under cover. He was shooting uphill as fast as he could lever a Winchester. Near Fargo, Roaring Tom grunted, went down. Fargo hesitated. "Go on!" the old man bellowed. "I jest caught it in the laig!"

Fargo changed direction, shotgun up. He ran hunched low, heading for the nest of boulders. Then Gordon saw him coming, and his voice rose again. "Fargo! Damn you, Neal, I mighta known!" He threw away an empty Winchester, whipped both Colts from their holsters. Fargo saw them come into line; he landed hard, skidding on his chest, as the slugs raked over him, fired the shotgun as he hit. Its right barrel sent a spray of slugs screaming off the rocks and Gordon dodged back unhit. His men had rallied, now, and were pumping rounds uphill toward the charging mountaineers, who were firing steadily and shattering the air with high, eerie rebel yells and hunter's calls. The dozen dogs still left alive were doing terrible work among the gunmen. Fargo saw one bowled over as a hound hit him from behind. Before he could recover, the dog's jaws were in his throat. Then a hound ran past Fargo, headed straight for the boulder where Lin Gordon crouched. With his eyes on Fargo, Gordon could not possibly see it coming.

The dog flashed behind the rock, a leaping blur of black and tan. Fargo scrambled to his feet, thumbing in a fresh round as he ran. He was within forty yards of the rock when Gordon, the dog's jaws fastened on his left arm, scrambled out, dragging the hound with

146

him. He whipped the Colt in his right hand around, fired; the dog fell, kicked once, and was dead. Then Gordon whirled; he saw Fargo coming on.

His face twisted. "You ruined it, Neal!" he yelled, blood streaming from his left forearm where the dog had mangled it. "You ruined it all! Even the show-down I had planned. But—" His teeth gleamed in his cadaverous face as he swung down the Colt and pulled the trigger.

Fargo rolled aside, loosed both shotgun barrels. Even as he did so, he heard the whine of Gordon's slug as it passed between arm and body. Then Gordon screamed, but it was cut off abruptly. Fargo broke the shotgun, staring in awe as he crammed in more shells.

There was almost nothing left of Gordon. The right barrel must have contained one of the chain shot shells he'd got from Roaring Tom. The left had held one of the rounds packed with birdshot in addition to the buck. At that range, all that lead and wire had chopped into Lin Gordon, and what fell limply bore no resemblance to a man. The head was half sliced off by piano wire.

"Judas," Fargo whispered. Then he had slugged in more rounds, snapped closed the gun, whirled just in time to punch the right barrel off at a gunman running toward him, trying to escape the hound pursuing him. The man went down, and the blood-maddened dog attacked his body. Suddenly, the valley was still except for a sudden spattering of fire from the direction of the pass, and the baying of the hounds.

Fargo let out a rasping breath, trying to fight off the battle-daze that gripped him. He blinked, looked around. The slope was littered with the bodies of men and dogs. He walked over to what was left of

147

Lin Gordon. He stared down at it. "Well," he said quietly, "now we'll never know who is best."

He turned away. The gunfire at the pass had died now. The guards had let that contingent through, then had taken them from the rear. It was over. Fargo went up the slope, to where Roaring Tom Canfield was coolly wrapping his shirt around his thigh to stop the flow of blood.

Up and down the slope, the dogs were flushing out the wounded and defeated, who came out with hands up, under the guns of the mountaineers. Fargo was glad to see that some had survived; their testimony would be needed. He looked down at Roaring Tom.

"Well," he said, "next stop Mexico."

Chapter IX

Three months later, Fargo entered the Regal Hotel in El Paso. It was not a particularly prepossessing place, but it was not a flophouse, either. Dressed in corduroy jacket, white shirt, tie, whipcord pants and polished cavalry boots, he might have been a prosperous cattleman in town for the weekend. The battered calvary hat was perched on the back of his head. The jacket's cut concealed the .38 shoulder-holstered under his left arm. He registered, then watched carefully as the bellhop carried the big trunk with its special lock into the elevator. It contained the shotgun, the Winchester, the Batangas knife, his bandoliers, and his spare ammunition. The twenty thousand dollars he had collected from Jim Hanna had long since been put in the bank.

The elevator doors closed behind the trunk. Fargo waited; there was not room in the small cubicle for him. "You have a Miss Bonnie Canfield registered here, right?" he asked the desk clerk.

"Yes, sir. She's in Room 210."

"Good," Fargo said. He turned away. Then, from across the lobby, a voice called his name.

He whirled instinctively, right hand half-moving across his body. Then he let it drop. "Hello, Mart," he said.

Mart Penny came toward him in broadbrimmed hat, town clothes, high-heeled boots, Ranger badge on his chest, Colt on his hip, under the coat. "You're jumpy," he grinned.

"I just came back from Mexico," Fargo said, as they shook hands.

"So you got the Canfields there all right?"

"They're settled in."

"Like the valley you took 'em to?"

"They liked it." Fargo paused, remembering how tears had run down Roaring Tom's cheeks at the sight of the wild, timbered splendor spread out below him. "They're there for good, unless the government wins the revolution—which they ain't got a prayer of doing. I used all my drag with Carranzo, Obregon and Villa to set it up."

"Which must be considerable. I'd like to hear about it. Can I buy you a drink?"

"Come up to my room," Fargo said. "There's a young lady upstairs who'll be waiting for the details, too."

"Sure." They got in the elevator. In Fargo's room, he unlocked the trunk, took out a fruit jar of clear liquid. Penny stared. "What's that?"

"Canfield corn. The last bottle left in the United States." Fargo grinned. "Come along."

He led Penny to Room 210, knocked on the door. In a moment, it opened. Bonnie Canfield stood there, eyes wide as she stared at Fargo.

He stared back. She was worth staring at—blond hair done in the latest fashion, the long, ugly gingham dress traded for something in colorful print and lace, hugging every line and curve of her figure. Then she whispered, "Fargo!" She threw herself at him, pressing her mouth against his. Only after the kiss was over did she see Penny; and when she did, she was not embarrassed. "Come in, come in," she said. "I've been waiting for you." Already, Fargo noticed, she had begun to lose her mountain twang.

"You look good. Not much like the hillbilly girl that rode out of Black Valley on my sorrel to pass the word to Hanna."

She smiled. "I learn fast. And I've got a job in a dress shop. That's one thing every Canfield woman really knows—how to sew clothes from start to finish." Then she was serious. "Fargo . . . When I . . . disappeared, on your horse . . . Daddy . . . How did he take it?"

"After I told him you were all right, he took it fine. He was anxious to get to Mexico, said if you wanted to leave the clan that bad, he wouldn't come looking for you."

"I know what else he said, too, I'll bet. That it was my mother's blood in me, like Jess, that I wasn't a true Canfield. That's why he didn't care. . . ."

"Maybe," Fargo said, but she had struck the truth. "Let her go," Roaring Tom had growled as the caravan had finally pulled out of Black Valley. "If she ain't enough Canfield to stay with her own fambly . . . I never should have married thet woman. She brought me nothing but grief, her and her spawn . . ."

"Tell me about about them," she said, after he had introduced Mart Penny. "Tell me everything that happened."

"It was a lot," Fargo said. "We wiped out Steed's gunfighters and didn't lose a man." He uncapped the fruit jar. "Lost some dogs and a few wounded. We lined up all the bodies, plus the prisoners, and we had just got through doing that when Jim Hanna came in with his herd. He pushed it through the pass, spread it out in the valley, and he and your daddy hit it off well, especially since Hanna paid the Canfields mighty generously to give up their claim on that valley."

"I see."

"Then Steed showed up, wondering what had happened to his gunmen. He clear about went out of his head when he saw most of 'em dead, and he began to threaten all kinds of things. Murder warrants, bringing in the army, that sort of stuff. Was gonna use his influence in the government to put all the Canfields in jail for murder. Jim Hanna squelched that in a hurry. He's got more influence than Steed ever dreamed about; he's been around a long time. He put Steed down, and hard. And nothin' Stead could do about it; Hanna had Black Valley and he didn't dare fight Hanna, even if he coulda rounded up another army. He rode out with his tail between his legs; especially since all those prisoners were left alive to testify against him as to how he had taken the law in his own hands."

"He'll have all the trouble he can deal with over that," Penny said.

"Anyhow, Jim Hanna made the arrangements for your folks to cross the border, embargo or no. He had to go to the governor and the adjutant general to do it. But the adjutant general himself hotfooted over there to see what was up." Fargo grinned, looked at Penny. "Jess wasn't the only one we saved you trouble on. It turned out that most of those gunslicks had warrants out on 'em. The Canfields wiped out about half of the badmen left in Texas. That didn't exactly made the adjutant general unhappy—especially since he's also commandant of

154

the Rangers. Cleaned up a lot of cases—and didn't cost the state a nickel or a Ranger's life."

"So you kept your end of the bargain with me and more," Penny said quietly. "Thanks, Neal. I knew you would."

"What bargain?" Bonnie asked quickly. Then she understood. "Oh . . . Jess."

"Jess. I'm sorry, ma'am," Penny said.

"Don't be," said Bonnie fiercely. "He had it coming to him. He was crazy. Mean crazy. I hated him . . . everybody hated him . . ." She broke off, then, sat down quickly on the bed. "He was my brother, but—never mind. It's over. Finished. He never existed."

Penny arose. "Neal, we're still down on the border. But I'll be around here a day or two, and we'll talk over old times." His eyes met Fargo's. "Actually, you see, we don't have enough men. There are places along the Rio we never patrol. It's not right, of course, but there are gaps in our line that if one of those gunrunners knew where they were, he could slip a whole train of mules through without our ever finding out. When you and the young lady have had your get-together, look me up. I'll buy you a drink and we'll talk about the Rio."

"Sure, Mart. Speaking of drinks—" Fargo held out the fruit jar. "Before you go, try that."

Penny took it, drank long and deeply, lowered it with a sigh of satisfaction. "Man," he said, in admiration. "That's drinkin' whiskey. If Mexico's the only place it's available from now on, I think I'll go down and join up with Villa." Then he grinned and left.

When the door closed behind him, Bonnie looked at Fargo for a moment. "I've been waiting for you so long. I thought you would never come."

"I'm here," said Fargo, and he took a long drink of Canfield corn and set the jar aside.

Bonnie's eyes were lambent. Her red lips curved. "El Paso's a wonderful town. I've learned a lot here. It's a real education for a mountain girl like me."

Fargo grinned. "I'll see if I can't help you continue your education," he said softly. And as he went to her, she came eagerly to meet him.

Three Complete Western Novels:

THREE COMPLETE
WESTERN NOVELS

Gun Brat
Wes Yancey

Breed Blood
Ben Jefferson

A Renegade Rides
Lee Floren

Price: $2.75 0-505-51788-4
Category: Western

Triple Western

Three action-packed, rip-roaring
adventure classics, by three of the
greatest Western writers ever to
tame the wild frontier!

SPRINGFIELD .45-70

Springfield .45-70

John Reese

Price: $1.95 0-505-51789-2
Category: Western

Madman with a Mad Gun

Raitt was a killer with a big grudge against the world.
Now he was out to get repaid for his suffering. First
he'd kill rancher Mike Banterman and steal the payroll
money. With his .45-70 he figured there'd be no stop-
ping him. Power, women, money—his for the taking!

Day of the Scorpion
Gene Shelton

Price: $2.25 0-505-51787-6
Category: Western

The Hunter and the Hunted

The Apaches called him the Scorpion, and he was itching to show the vicious Henderson gang the deadly sting of revenge. The outlaws had raided his farm and murdered his wife. Now the Scorpion had to search the rocky desert for traces of the killers, knowing that he couldn't rest until his wife had been avenged and the last drop of blood had been shed.

"Your fault. Kept me awake almost all night," she told him, her answering smile sensuous. "I have to get some rest sometime."

"When we get back home, I'll let you get some rest."

Going home. The thought scared her. As she looked into his emerald eyes, her expression altered and became serious. "When we do get back, are you going to move back into your apartment in Raleigh? I mean, if you don't think Vincent Keaton's a danger anymore?"

"Do you want me to move out of your house?"

"I'm asking you. Do you want to?"

"No. I'd like to stay, Micki."

"Why?" she questioned, eagerly gathering up all her courage. "Debbie told me I should ask you if you love me. Do you?"

He raised his eyebrows. "Let me ask you the same thing. Do you love me?"

"Y-yes, I do," she said, her voice catching. "Very much."

"Then say it."

"I love you, Jon," she whispered, running her hand up his left arm, her nails catching in fine dark hairs. "I love you so much."

Her caress made him tremble. His eyes darkened. "And I love you, Micki, more than I can ever say."

He took her in his arms, and she went to him with joyful tears springing to her eyes. "And you said you were afraid of making a commitment. You lied to me."

"No, I didn't. You just overcame my defenses," he murmured, nuzzling her ear with his lips, aroused by the fragrance and feel of her. "Let's go inside, Micki."

"I thought you wanted to swim."

"I changed my mind," he said, getting to his feet and pulling her up with him. Together they walked arm-in-arm up to the beach bungalow they were renting. Bougainvillaea vines laced the stucco walls, and the brilliant scarlet flowers shimmered in the sunlight.

Inside the bungalow he urgently stripped off her swimsuit and his own trunks and carried her to bed, passion running wild in him. "I love you. Love you. Love you," he whispered gruffly as he ran his hands all over her slender, shapely body.

"Love you, too. Oh Jon, I do," she breathed, accompanying her words with wanton caresses, feeling closer to him than she ever had. When they could wait no longer for the ultimate intimacy and their bodies united, she softly cried out, and her cry mingled with his groan of pleasure as their mouths merged together.

After the loving, Michelle lay wrapped in Jon's arms on the cool sheet and rubbed her chin lightly against his hair-roughened chest. Suddenly she felt brave, unafraid. "If you're willing to make enough of a commitment to live with me, why don't we just make it legal and get married? We could buy a house somewhere between Raleigh and Chapel Hill so neither of us has to drive so far to work. What'd you say?"

He pulled back slightly so he could look at her face. "What's this, woman? Are you proposing to me? I thought you were the one who didn't like to rush things?"

She smiled winningly. "Well, we love each other. Why not get married?"

One corner of his mouth tilted up. "This is a big decision, Micki. I'm going to have to think it over."

"Well, think fast, Mr. Wyatt," she warned coquettishly, "or I might change my mind."

"A house in the country between Chapel Hill and Raleigh," he said musingly a few seconds later. "I have to admit it sounds appealing. Our house, Micki. All right, you talked me into it. Marry me?"

"Thought you'd never ask," she said, happiness filling her heart as she cuddled closer to him and brushed a kiss over the side of his neck. "Of course, this means you have to buy me an engagement ring soon. Debbie will be disappointed if you don't."

"Can't take a chance on disappointing her. How big a diamond do you want? Just remember I'm no millionaire."

"You're not?" She pretended to be surprised. "Then I don't know if I want to marry you after all."

"Just try to back out now, woman!" he warned, pulling her over on top of him, sweeping his hands slowly over her naked back. Trembling, she kissed him. "Micki, my sweet love," he whispered, wrapping his arms around her, "how many children do you think we should have?"

"Now you really are rushing things," she answered, her lips curving in a smile against his. "You've always been such an aggressive man."

"And you like me that way."

"Yes," she quite willingly agreed. "I like you that way. I love you that way."

"Love you, too, Micki," he uttered roughly, his warm mouth swiftly covering hers.

Michelle sighed happily. She had waited for the right man and had found him. That made her an extremely lucky woman.